IN POSSESSION OF A GOOD FORTUNE

A PEMBERLEY RANCH ROMANCE BOOK 3

SHANAE JOHNSON

THOSE JOHNSON GIRLS

Edited by Kasi Alexander

"There is nothing so manly as a bull rider," Lydia Bennett sighed as she eyed the man candy striding around the Pemberley Ranch grand ball room.

For most of the year, the Darcys' large manor home was mostly vacant, not admitting guests. But once each year, sour-faced Fitz Darcy would open his home for a few weeks of revelry that included a horse auction, a beauty pageant and a rodeo and culminated in a grand ball.

Currently, the grand ballroom was filled with men in denim that showcased nicely rounded riding gear in the back. The men's long legs were encased in leather chaps that did not detract from their strong muscles. Each six foot plus frame was capped with a well-worn cowboy hat that cast devilish shadows beneath dark and brooding eyes.

Unfortunately, those shadows made it hard to catch any of the bull riders' gazes. Perhaps, Lydia thought, if she unknotted the scarf around her neck and dropped it on the floor, then surely one of the riders would bend down and pick it up. Then, when he rose to hand it back to her, he'd definitely have to look into her eyes and introduce himself.

"Lydia, you are such a flirt." Her best friend Emma gave her a playful shove.

Oops, she had said that out loud without meaning to. Still, Lydia had been called worse than a flirt. Her eldest sister Jane called her untamed. Their middle sister Eliza called her unabashed, a word Lydia had to look up in the dictionary. It meant not embarrassed. Which she wasn't. She didn't have anything to be embarrassed for.

She was a woman grown. Just turned twenty-one. Completely legal and ready to mingle. Though most men in Austen Valley were more interested in mingling with her bestie than they were with her.

Along with being an heiress, Emma Woodhouse was model gorgeous. With her long gazelle-like legs and her swan's neck, the woman could've passed for Tyra Bank's younger, more attractive sister. Men were always falling over themselves for her.

Em wasn't classically beautiful. She was ethereal. Someone had once called her handsome. Lydia had thought it an insult before she'd looked the word up in her trusty dictionary. In the dictionary, there were two entries for the word. One was for men, the other for women. The definition for women noted that the word meant someone who was striking in their looks rather than pretty.

That was Em: handsome, clever, and rich.

Lydia could only claim the second one on that list. She knew she wasn't unattractive. She got enough attention on her own to confirm it. But most of that attention came because she stood in the castoff of Emma's glow. Lydia's wits were the most notable thing about her, and she used to them to great effect, getting information out of people and writing about it on her blog.

But the third characteristic? Rich? Nope. While the Bennetts weren't poor, they held a precarious hold on their middle class status. Em had grown up rich and was set to inherit more money than she could ever hope to spend in just a matter of months when she turned twenty-one.

"I heard that Giana Fairfax was caught in the saddle with a rider last night," said Emma, her head dipped to Lydia's ear to ensure no one would hear.

That caught Lydia's attention. In addition to being called a flirt, the term gossip had also attached itself to Lydia. The funny part about that was that the term had never latched on to Emma, who was always the bearer of juicy news. Lydia supposed the reason the unkind term attached to her instead of Emma was because it was Lydia who was often responsible for spreading the news that Emma told her.

"Goody Two-shoes Giana? No, I don't believe it." Lydia gripped her best friend's arm and pulled her even closer, eager to hear more of the potentially scandalous story.

Potentially because Lydia actually didn't believe any of it was true. She knew enough of Giana Fairfax's character to know that the young woman had likely been in the barn to return a saddle than she was there to ride anything—or anyone. For whatever reason, Emma wanted the tidbits about Giana spread over town, and because Emma knew Lydia's character, she knew that her best friend wouldn't be able to help but repeat what she'd been told.

Most gossip held a kernel of truth. Lydia had developed a knack for parsing out the facts from the fiction. The problem was very few people were interested in the facts.

It was great fodder for her blog, *Austentatious*. Though she wrote about the goings on of the small town of Austen Valley, she had over twenty-five thousand hits on her blog each month. Her recent posts about Telenovela star turned rancher Carlos Bingley had gained her international notice and bumped her up to thirty thousand. Though now that he was going to be her brother-in-law, Lydia supposed she had to stop snooping in on his and her sister's conversations. Or at least ask before she posted any deets about them.

"Excuse me, ma'am."

Lydia jerked her ear away from Emma as one of the bull riders broke from the pack and sidled up to her. She brushed her red pixie locks from her green eyes and put on her brightest, most flirtatious smile. She smoothed a hand down her sundress, meeting with a snag at the waist where Jane had let out the fabric to fit her curves.

The dress had belonged to Emma, but Lydia had rescued the garment from Em's donation bag a couple weeks ago. Em was forever wearing the latest fashions and tossing them out after one wear. Lydia always volunteered to drive the articles to the local Goodwill, often liberating a few garments along the way. She was glad she'd freed this dress and altered it to fit her form with the handsome bull rider approaching.

With a flick of his finger, the bull rider tipped up his cowboy hat, releasing the shadows from his blue eyes. Lydia's pulse bucked, like a bull let out of the gate. Only to come to a crashing halt when she realized that blue gaze wasn't on her, but Emma.

Of course it was.

"Beg your pardon," said the cowboy, flashing white teeth at Em as he drawled, "but you have got to be the prettiest girl in here, and I had to introduce myself. I'm Denny."

"I'm Emma. And this is my friend Lydia."

"Hmm," Denny said with barely a cursory glance at Lydia. "I heard Austen Valley was known for its steak house restaurants. I thought you'd like to take me out to the best one tonight."

"You want me to take you out?" Emma snorted.

"Well, yes, ma'am," said Denny, removing his cowboy hat to let his blond locks fall into those blue eyes. "You see, I'm a feminist. I believe in equality."

Em slid her glance to Lydia, who met it with wary amusement. There were a lot of male feminists who'd made themselves known to Emma over the years. A better term for them was gold-digger.

"Feminists advocate for women's rights," said a deep male voice. "They don't put more burdens on the fairer sex."

Denny's smile faltered in the face of George Knightley. Though Knightly was only ten years older than the two of them, just barely on the other side of thirty, he had a shock of gray on one side of his jet-black hair. That wisdom streak didn't make him look any older, but it certainly made him act an advanced age.

Emma, on the other hand, got *that look* on her face when Knightly stepped in to interfere. It was the narrow-eyed look of a woman who wanted a man's attention but didn't want that man to know she gave him a single thought. If Knightly told Emma the sky was blue, she'd insist it was green. If he told her to stand up, she'd sit down.

"I'm having a party this weekend," Emma said with a bright smile for the gold-digger. "You should come."

Denny's smile was one hundred karats of fake gold bright. He reached out a hand for her. Before he could overstep his bounds, Knightly cut him off. The severe look made the man who rode bulls for a living back down. Denny tipped his hat, risked another grin at Emma, and then shuffled off.

"You know that man is only after one thing," said Knightly.

"Aren't they all?" said Emma with a roll of her eyes. "We're just having fun, Knightly. Something you've clearly forgotten how to do in your old age."

Emma crossed her arms over her chest, a clear sign that she was settling in for a long argument with Knightly. Knightly planted himself in front of the young woman and peered down at her disapprovingly. The two were in for one of their battle of wills. They wouldn't have noticed if Lydia walked off. Except Lydia noticed that Knightly hadn't come over alone.

The thin man trying to look as though he wasn't interested in the *tete*—another word Lydia had to look up—taking place in front of him looked familiar. Though Knightly was consummately proper, it didn't look like he was going to introduce them. It was the label on the pen in his hand that jogged Lydia's memory, causing her to go into action.

"Emma was helping me," she said to Knightly. "I'm doing research for a story I'm writing on bull riders. An exposé, actually. I'm looking at how the men use pick-up lines and chase after women. My readers are going to love it."

The as-yet-to-be-introduced man's eyes perked up. It wasn't in the way Lydia had hoped Denny's eyes had taken an interest in her. But she didn't want to date this man. She wanted to work for him.

"You're a reporter?" asked the man.

"I am," said Lydia. Though she was technically a blogger.

"My apologies," said Knightly, finally releasing his glare on Emma and finding his manners. "Dawson Perry, this is Lydia Bennett. Lydia, this is my friend Dawson. He's the editorial director of the *Austen Capitol* newspaper."

"Nice to meet you, Ms. Bennett."

"Please, call me Lydia."

"You didn't say which news outlet you wrote for, Lydia."

Lydia held on to her grin so that she didn't twist her lip and thereby twist the truth. She might turn facts into fiction on her blog, but what she really wanted was to write creative nonfiction for a reputable newspaper.

"I write for *Austentatious*," she said, letting go of her lip and tilting up her head.

Mr. Perry wrinkled his nose at the mention of her site. "That homemade gossip page written by some juvenile?"

"It's a blog—my blog, in fact." Lydia's head tilted higher, staring straight on at Mr. Perry. "It gets over thirty thousand views a month. And I'm a college graduate with a degree in journalism."

"Thirty thousand hits, you say?" Mr. Perry's brows perked up at the number.

There was a touch of gray at his temples. Clearly, he wasn't her demographic, but his readers could be. The *Capitol* newspaper didn't have a gossip column. Lydia was convinced that was a major reason why circulation was going down. Gossip was a hallmark of human communication.

In college, she'd read a statistic that sixty percent of humans gossiped. It wasn't just for entertainment purposes. There was real value in listening to and spreading hearsay. Indulging in the chatter of what came down the grapevine brought news of whom to trust and who to avoid, how resources fared, and lessons of survival. In truth, gossip was one of the highest forms of social intelligence.

"Tell me more about the story you're working on at present," said Mr. Perry.

"I… um…"

The switch from disdain to interest caught Lydia off guard. From the corner of her eye, she saw Denny approach another bull rider. It was clear this man was a rider, even though he didn't wear any leather over his well-fitted jeans. There were no spurs on his boots. His cowboy hat was pulled low on his head, but it was clear this man had been ridden hard in his life. The cords of the muscles along his forearms showed that he'd held on tightly, and he wasn't quite done fighting.

"Bull riders," Lydia heard herself murmuring. "I'm doing an exposé on bull riders."

"On the rodeo?" Mr. Perry asked, the interest leaking from his voice once more.

"No. Not the rodeo. Who cares about the rodeo? Anybody who comes to the rodeo comes for the riders."

Lydia's attention again turned to the two bull riders standing in the corner. Her gaze quickly slipped from Denny and slid to his friend; the dark and brooding man leaning against the wall. He was standing so powerful on those strong thighs that it looked he alone was holding up the halls of Pemberley.

"We want to know the intricate details of their lives—their private lives, not just their public face. Who they love. What they've lost. What they hunger for."

As though he heard her speaking, the bull rider in question lifted his head and found her gaze. His dark eyes robbed her of breath as he held her stare. But the stare only lasted for a second before his gaze shifted to take in Emma.

Lydia deflated, like a balloon that had been held together by the string. All the air inside her gushed out, leaving her feeling lightheaded.

"You think you can get that story?" asked Mr. Perry.

She had to blink a couple of times and take a deep breath before speaking. "I'm going to get that story."

"When you have a draft, I'd love to see it."

Lydia blinked. Her focus returned to Mr. Perry. Was he offering her a job? She didn't have a chance to ask. Mr. Perry turned his back and disappeared into the crowded ballroom.

Once again, Lydia's mouth had spread news that only held a kernel of truth in it. She hadn't been planning to write anything about the bull riders. She wasn't even sure if her readers would be interested. But now she'd have to do a story on the topic. She just had to find a bull rider to expose.

CHAPTER TWO

George Wickham leaned against the back wall in the grand ball. His stance was casual, and the long, lean lines of his body gave off all the appearance of a man relaxed without a care in the world. Behind his back, his fingers fidgeted as he checked, again and again, the distance he was to the door of the back patio.

He was close enough to the exit that if he saw security coming, he could get out before being marched out like the last time he was here. He pursed his lips and shoved that memory away. It was a long time ago.

Things were different now. He didn't work for the Darcys any longer. He was no longer at their financial whim.

No, he was at another person's whim these days. But such was the life of everyone not born into piles of old money.

Speaking of old money, Wick's eyes tracked the location of the dark-haired man that stood heads and shoulders above all who'd gathered. Fitz Darcy had not yet noticed his former employee's presence in his home. If Darcy had, Wick was certain he never would've made it past the main gate.

There had been a misunderstanding years ago. Wick

had been summarily dismissed from his position at Pemberley and warned never to return again. Yet here he was drinking the man's wine, breathing the rare air of the wealthy, and rubbing elbows with the cream of Austen Valley's crop.

Though the elbow-rubbing wasn't actually happening. Wick knew that if he dared take a few more steps into the room, Darcy would spot him and toss him out on his backside. Much like their last encounter, which had happened nearly ten years ago over a girl.

"Wickham, what are you doing in the back like a wallflower?"

Benjamin Denny's voice boomed up into the vaulted ceilings. The sound carried across the ballroom. For one instance, Darcy's shoulders tensed, and Wick was certain he'd been found out.

But then that haughty, superior gaze fell onto a young woman in the crowd. A redhead who had her head thrown back in laughter and amusement. The intense gaze Darcy landed on the girl made Wick doubt that even if Darcy had heard his name, it wouldn't have registered.

Interesting. So the heartless man was in love? And the object of his affection wasn't fawning all over him? Served the villain right.

Love made fools of any who dared reach for it. He'd seen the bloody red carnage the heart spilled more times than he cared to count. It was an endeavor Wick knew he'd never undertake.

"I just got us an invite to a house party this weekend," Denny was saying.

"We have a rodeo to ride in this weekend," said Wick. "We don't have time to party."

Hearing the words come out of his mouth made Wick feel ancient. At the ripe old age of twenty-eight, he felt he was already past his prime as a bull rider. His body was certainly all over that argument.

Even now, his knee protested his long-held stance leaning against the wall. But Wick dared not venture farther into the house he used to call a home. Not even when his lower back joined in on the complaint.

Though the ordeal only lasted for eight seconds at a turn, bull riding was murder on the body. It was no wonder with a fifteen hundred-pound angry beast pitching a fit as it insisted the unwanted rider get off its back.

Still, it was the profession Wick loved. The only profession he'd even been remotely interested in as a kid. He'd gotten to the top of the field... until it all came crashing down.

"I can't believe the party animal of the rodeo, the Brazen Bull himself, says he doesn't have time to party," said Denny.

The former party animal had to be on his best game for the rodeo this weekend. Wick needed that prize money, even if only to put a dent in the debts that were threatening to drown him.

"The beauty queens will be there," said Denny.

At another time, that would've been a tempting ploy for Wick. Pageant princesses were accomplished women dolled up in expensive gowns. Those gowns meant they or their families had money to burn on useless talents and outrageous dresses. A wealthy girlfriend would be just the thing to put another dent in his debts. Or maybe erase them entirely. But inevitably women would want a piece of his heart, and that was something Wick planned never give to anyone.

"The girl that's hosting is set to inherit millions on her twenty-first birthday," Denny went on.

Wick's hand let go of his lower back, and the ache slipped from his attention. His body came off the wall, going erect to his full height. Millions would not only erase his debt, it could set him up for life. It could even afford him the necessary heart surgery to place an object into the black cavern that was inside his chest so that he could fake some feelings. Millions of dollars were worth at least one look at the woman.

"Who?" Wick asked.

With a triumphant grin, Denny pointed a finger. Wick followed the trajectory of that finger to a young woman with fiery red hair that looked like flames. The sight of it sent a bead of sweat running between Wick's shoulder blades.

Another man stood in front of her. A thin, reedy specimen of a man. Wick's right hand curled into a fist. Blood pumped from his chest and down into his palm. That fire in his veins urged him to march over there and remove the interloper bodily from the redhead. Why? Because he was obstructing Wick's view of her. Because he was standing too close to her.

Then she lifted her gaze to him, and Wick's knees, already embattled from too many throws from a bull, went completely weak. The light in her green eyes washed out the bawdy sequins the pageant princesses wore. It even dimmed the chandelier. Her lips stretched into a broad smile. That smile said that, like every entitled heiress he'd ever encountered, she was a woman used to getting everything she wanted.

"It's her," Wick murmured. Along with the murmur from his lips, his vacant heart made a whooshing sound like when he was on the back of a bull nearing the final second of an eight-second ride when he was about to be bucked off and tossed down on his backside.

"Yep," said Denny. "That's her. That's Emma Woodhouse."

Wick's gaze shifted past the redhead and her friend to a figure moving toward them. Fitzwilliam Darcy was getting closer to his side of the ballroom. The man still hadn't seen him yet, but Wick could no longer spare him a care. Not when he saw the solution to all of his problems wrapped up in a red, hot, curvy bundle.

The Idea was mounted in his head. He felt the bull rope being wrapped securely around his palm. A bell chimed in his head over and over again, announcing the start of something epic.

George Wickham was going to make Emma Woodhouse his before the night was over.

CHAPTER THREE

*L*ydia reached into her purse for her pink Energel pen. She used to be a fan of the Inkjet pens, but after the pink bleed at the bottom of her Kate Spade purse last year, the purse being another cast-off from Em, she had quickly switched to the more secure Pentel line.

Leaving Em, who was still arguing with Knightly about her flirty tendencies, Lydia walked over to an empty corner of the ballroom. She pressed the end cap at the top of the pen to let down the tip, and the writing utensil made a satisfying clicking sound. That sound indicated that she meant business. The pink ink glided smoothly onto the dotted paper of her bullet journal, or bujo, as she began to write her plan of action to gather and then expose the deepest, darkest secrets of one of the bull riders here at the Pemberley Rodeo this weekend.

An exposé article was much like an expository essay. It would start with a gathering of the facts, which needed to include anecdotes and quotations and descriptive details. But instead of charts and statistics, the exposé would need photos that could be left open to the interpretation of the reader. An interpretation that was helped along by well-formulated questions and well-placed gaps of information composed by the writer.

Lydia snagged a roll of washi tape from her planner pouch. She unraveled a length and placed it at the top edge of the blank page in her bujo. The decorative tape lined the edge of the page to indicate the start of a new story. She simply couldn't start without the decoration. She had to make the page pretty in order to receive the delicious details to help her write.

She was sure most journalists didn't use craft items to help them organize. But she wasn't a journalist. She was an opinionist. There was a difference.

Her hero, Wendy Williams, had made her millions off her nosiness and her gift of gab. Lydia saw no reason why she couldn't do the same. Except that this was a small town. Though she'd found that the residents here often held the best stories, because people thought no one was watching. But Lydia was always watching.

"Miss Bennett."

Lydia looked up sharply. While she'd been hiding in a corner, she'd been caught unaware by the most busy-bodied person in all the valley. She turned with reluctance to come face to face with the lady of Pemberley Manor, Mrs. Catherine Darcy DeBourgh.

"Now, now, missy," Ms. Catherine started in. "I don't want any mention of our guests in that little email of yours."

Lydia had tried to explain to Ms. Catherine that she wrote blogs, not emails. Blogs stayed on the Internet where an email was sent and could be discarded by the end user. "I'm writing a piece about the rodeo—"

Ms. Catherine jabbed a gnarled finger into the air.

"—for *The Capitol* newspaper," Lydia managed to finish

despite the silent shot fired into the air by that weaponized digit.

Ms. Catherine's finger bent at the knuckle, and she arched an eyebrow.

Lydia envied her that. She envied anyone who could raise a single brow. Whenever she tried to do it, it looked like she had something in her eye.

"It surprises me that a serious newspaper would have someone who's more interested in arts and crafts write a story." Ms. Catherine's finger went erect again as it pointed at Lydia's decorated bujo.

Lydia brought her journal to her chest and opened her mouth to make a retort, but Ms. Catherine wasn't done.

"Out of all of your sisters, you're most like your mother."

Lydia squeezed her journal into her thumping heart. She'd learned the art of bullet journaling and crafting from her mother. After she'd passed away, Lydia had found her mother's journals. They'd been filled with the juiciest gossip about all of her mother's friends in the town. Her mother's words had been so conversational, so engaging, that Lydia had wanted to mimic them and began a journal of her own. Pretty soon, she'd wanted others to read her words, and her blog was born.

"Your mother was a gossip too. But at least she kept her chatter to the kitchen table instead of writing it down and sending it out in emails."

"It's not emails. It's-"

"I thought you'd be an obedient miss. But then you got your father's red hair."

Lydia self-consciously touched her curls. Her hair was the darkest shade of red of all the Bennett girls. It was auburn, a shade that touched brown but still held on to the vibrancy of red. With her preferred short style, she was often told it made her look like a fairy. A deranged fairy, a few had said just within earshot. But she chose to focus only on the word *fairy*.

"You should consider keeping your chatter to the kiddie table. Until you have permission to speak with the adults."

And with that, Ms. Catherine was off.

It was a set-down. An excellent set-down. No one could keep it classy while putting a person in their place like Catherine Darcy DeBourgh.

But Lydia wasn't about to sit down or hold still. This was her chance to be taken as a serious journalist and not just a gossip. She wanted her opinion to matter, and it would if she could get published in a reputable paper. To do that, she'd need to wrangle a bull rider.

"Oh, good, she's gone," Eliza said as she stepped out of another corner, eyeing Ms. Catherine's retreating back.

Though the woman was in her seventies, Ms. Catherine moved like a young general commanding a vast army. As she stormed through the ballroom, men, women, and children all leaped out of her way, staring warily after her.

"If I thought Darcy was a trial, a moment alone with that woman is worse than a death sentence," said Eliza.

"Thanks for your rescue, sis," Lydia said, her voice dripping with sarcasm over her sister's late arrival.

Eliza turned her hunter green eyes on Lydia. Her bone-straight hair could be called strawberry blond, but Lydia had always thought it was more the color of an apple than a strawberry.

"Whatever." Eliza shrugged. "You should be thankful I never uploaded any of the Photoshopped pictures of you and Justin Bieber that you made."

Lydia pressed her lips together to hold in her gasp, but a huff of indignation still escaped her nose. Having two sisters was more often than not the worst.

"Anyway," said Eliza, waving her hand in the air as though

brushing away the dig she had just made, "I need your help with the horses."

"I'm in the middle of something."

Eliza looked over her shoulder and spotted the bull riders. "You can flirt with them all weekend."

"I'm not going to flirt with anyone."

Eliza raised a dubious eyebrow. This was likely where Lydia had learned to dislike the facial expression.

"The horses are not my job. I'm a writer."

"You're a blogger."

The way her sister correctly named Lydia's chosen profession made it sound even lower than when Ms. Catherine had incorrectly stated it. Did no one respect the valuable work she did?

"Fine," Eliza huffed. "Go tell your stories. Just don't sneak around Pemberley. The last thing I need is to deal with Darcy."

Lydia knew the only thing her sister wanted to do was deal with Fitz Darcy. But neither Eliza nor Darcy could bring themselves to admit the truth of that well-known fact.

"And for the love of all things," said Eliza, turning back to face her younger sister, "don't do something silly like drop your scarf, hoping for one of the cowboys to pick it up. That is so cliché."

That had been her plan a few moments ago. It had seemed sound. But now that Eliza ridiculed it, it sounded stupid.

She heard Eliza's laughter trickle as she disappeared out one of the side doors. Lydia turned from her sister with a huff. When she did, the roll of washi tape she'd been using slipped from her hands. It rolled across the floor and into the circle of riders. Until it was stopped by a well-worn cowboy boot.

Lydia looked up, and then up some more, until she came

face to face with the owner of that boot. He bent his muscled body down to scoop up the tape. He had long, nimble fingers that made the decorative tape appear like it would fit any of his fingers as a ring.

When the cowboy straightened, he seemed even taller. His mouth split into a grin. "Beg your pardon, ma'am, but I think you dropped this."

It was the same bull rider who'd been standing with Denny a few moments ago. The one who had looked past her to check out Emma. He was looking at her now, likely thinking she would get him close to Emma. Well, he'd be sorely disappointed on that front. She was in no mood to be used. But she could do a bit of using in the meantime.

It looked like Lydia had found her man. This was going to be easy.

CHAPTER FOUR

ick didn't have sisters. His mother had abandoned him soon after he'd learned to call for her by using that title. He'd always supposed since his first word was *dada* and not *mama* that she'd taken offense to the slight and left. All that to say that he hadn't grown up around girlish things, so when the odd roll of tape spun up to his boot, he wasn't sure what to make of it.

He bent to pick up the object. There were flowers and hearts along the front face of it. At the borders were gold foil. The actual material appeared to be tape, but what it was made of appeared flimsy. He doubted it could hold anything together. Perhaps it wasn't even tape after all?

It was pretty to look at. Much like its owner. No, not pretty. Emma Woodhouse was a breathtakingly beautiful young woman.

Wick looked up into her bright green eyes from his perch, low to the ground. That fiery red hair was like a halo of flames coming toward him as he straightened. The closer he got to her, the more he was certain he was being scorched from the inside out.

The burn was good. It warmed the icy cage around his internal organs, namely the one inside his chest. So he kept stalking closer and closer to her.

She made no move to come to him. She stood like a gazelle staring down at the lion, preparing to devour her. Instead of shrinking in fear, she smiled up at him.

That smile made Wick miss a step. He quickly recovered and strode the last step to come toe to toe with her. When he reached her, she held out her hand to him, palm open.

Wick's most pressing instinct was to recoil. But that was only because his first instinct was to lay his thawing heart in her hands and sink to his knees in reverence. Soon enough, he came to his senses and realized it wasn't his soul she was asking for, but the roll of tape.

"Do you use this to stitch broken hearts back together?" he asked, twirling the tape on his finger.

"Broken hearts?"

Her voice was silky and smooth. He felt the tips of his ears heat at the sound of it. He was standing a foot away from her, but he leaned in when he spoke again. All so he could hear her sultry voice clearer.

"Yes, broken hearts," he said. "Of all the men left in your trail."

Her smile had only lifted on one side of her mouth. Now it spread to both sides. Wick couldn't hide his gasp when she flashed perfect white teeth at him. Her head tilted back slightly as she let out a sound of delight.

His mind went blank for a full second. When he came to, the only thought running through his head was how to get her to make that sound again.

"It's washi."

"Washi?" he repeated.

"It's decorative tape." She pointed to the roll around his finger. "It couldn't hold an organ together or patch one up."

"Decorative?" He pinched the tape between his fingers, noting the fact that she still had her hand outstretched to him. "What do you use it for, then?"

She held up a journal in her other hand. Using her thumb, she flipped the cover open to a random page inside. Wick caught a glimpse of the foiled tape at the top of the page before she slammed the book closed.

Ah. This was much more familiar to him. A rich woman with secrets. This brought her back into the realm of what he knew to be true of her class. Secrets he could deal with. Lord knows he had enough of his own.

"I use it to make things pretty," she said.

Wick's gaze slid over her features once more. The wide green eyes that reminded him a spring day in the open pastures. The silky red tresses that brought to mind the fall of maple leaves. That porcelain skin that made him want to bring her close and wrap her up on a cold winter's night.

"I don't see why someone as beautiful as you would need to make anything prettier."

A warm blush spread across her cheeks, bringing him back to steamy summer nights in the valley. He took a step closer, feeling heat begin to blossom across his chest.

"When I meet someone new, I like to find out about them," she said. "The washi helps me to organize my thoughts."

"You keep all your thoughts in there?" Wick asked, indicating the book.

She placed the journal behind her back with one hand and then snatched the roll of tape from his finger with the other. It was only a brief contact, and only from the tips of her thumb and index finger. Still, Wick felt fire blaze through him. Sweat beaded on his brow and between his shoulder blades as the cold recess of his inner world continued to melt at a rapid pace.

What was it about this woman that she could illicit such a response from him?

"I'm someone new," he said. "Would you like to know more about me?"

"I would," she said, tucking the tape into a pouch Wick could see was filled with even more rolls of colorful tape and an assortment of pens.

"Ask away. I'm an open book."

"Tell me about the last time you were in love."

That was a splash of cold water on his face. In real time, the sweat on his forehead and back cooled. His chest constricted, giving over to the ever-present chill inside him.

"What?" she asked. "You don't believe in love?"

"Love makes fools of men."

"I think love makes fools of women more than men."

Wick shook his head. "Women get a little crush. Men fall and get hurt. That fall gives them deep wounds."

He had not meant to have a deep philosophical discussion about love with this particular woman. He was supposed to be sweeping her off her feet and making her believe he was falling for her. But here he stood toe to toe with her, telling her his true feelings about love instead of trying to convince her that he was fast developing those feelings for her.

"So you *have* been in love?" she asked.

"No," Wick said honestly. It was the last honest thing he planned to tell her. "But I have seen it."

"And after seeing it, you want no part in it?"

There was disappointment in her eyes. Wick didn't like it there. He wanted the playfulness back. He opened his mouth to lie, but once again, the truth threatened to come out. He cleared his throat and steered his tongue in a different direction.

"Do you want a part of it?" Wickham held his breath, waiting for her answer.

"Love makes the best stories," she said.

"Since I've never been in love, you think that means I don't have a story?"

"Everyone has a story. Do you want to tell me more about yours?"

Wick stared at her, trying to parse out exactly what she meant. He knew this conversation was being had on two levels. He just couldn't figure out what her angle was.

As though she'd heard him, she clarified. "Tell me the story of how you became a bull rider."

She was smiling, so she was definitely flirting. But she wasn't flipping her hair. She wasn't lifting her chest. She looked at him earnestly. She even had a pen poised in her hand as though she was going to start taking notes in that pretty little book of hers. He wanted to dig through her bag and pick out which of the colorful washi tapes she would use when she wrote about him in there.

What rich woman took notes on a potential lover? Maybe she had a thing for bull riders. She wouldn't be the first.

"But first," she said, ripping off a piece of the decorative tape and placing at the top of a blank page in her journal, "tell me your name."

"You can call me Wick."

"Hi, Wick. I'm—"

"Flame. I'm going to call you Flame."

CHAPTER FIVE

"Did you always know you wanted to be a bull rider?"

Lydia and Wick walked at a slow pace away from the manor. The sky had darkened, giving over to night. Lights along the paved drive illuminated the way as cars snaked down the road to leave Pemberley. The party inside the great house was over. Even the animals were settling down for the night. But Lydia was just getting started with her subject.

They stopped walking at the edge of a pen where a few bulls and broncs were out grazing. The animals looked entirely harmless, docile even with their heads bent low, intent on their meals. In just a few days' time, they would be leaping in the air, kicking furiously with the intention of bucking off anyone who dared cling to their backs.

Wick leaned against the wood railing of the enclosure and tipped his cowboy hat up. "I wasn't one of those kids that had any kind of a plan growing up."

"Me neither," Lydia admitted.

Unlike her sisters, who had come out of the womb

knowing exactly what they were meant to do, and were both now doing it, Lydia had come into this world babbling. She hadn't stopped talking since. With ads, her blog made her the same amount of money as waitressing, but not enough to move out and live on her own. Which was why she needed to impress the editor from the *Capitol*.

"You didn't know you wanted to be a writer?" Wick asked.

"How did you know I'm a writer?"

The rules of investigative journalism didn't require her to reveal herself to her subject. In fact, by keeping her true identity as a reporter secret, she was sure to get the juiciest details from him.

"With all those pens"—Wick pointed at her purse, which held her pen pouch—"I just assumed. Am I right?"

"I like talking to people and writing stories about what I hear." It was neither a confirmation nor a denial.

"To answer your question, I ride bulls because I'm good at it. I've always had a knack for taming wild things."

He reached for a lock of her hair. Bringing the red curl between his index and forefinger, he rubbed the tresses back and forth in a hypnotic motion. Once or twice, Lydia felt the caress of his warm, callused flesh against her cheek.

"I'm not a wild thing," she said, and her voice, which normally boomed, sounded tame to her ears.

"No?"

Wick let go of her hair. The lock bounced back in place, but not before springing up and down a couple of times. Lydia held the rest of her body still, feeling certain that if she didn't, she'd launch herself into him.

Then she did.

She leaned forward toward him. Wick's hand, which was still hanging in the air between them, wrapped around her chin. His thumb brushed her lower lip, then made gentle circles against her cheek.

It felt entirely natural. It felt entirely right. It felt like they'd been doing this their whole lives, even though they'd just met a quarter of an hour ago.

"It's dangerous," she said.

"Taming wild things?"

"Riding bulls."

"Hmm." He rested his other hand on her waist, pulling her closer to him. "It's also fun."

"Fun?"

"There's a pageantry to a rodeo."

"Yeah, it's kind of like the circus. There are even clowns."

"Those aren't clowns, Flame." He ran his fingers through her hair again, watching as the short tresses spilled across his palm like running water. "Those are bullfighters."

"They fight the bulls?"

He met her gaze, amusement shining brightly from within. "Are you sure you've been to a rodeo before?"

"I have," Lydia said, tilting up her chin. She just hadn't paid that much attention. Being up and close to this bull rider left her making a mental note of every detail. Normally, she would be writing it all down in her bujo. But Lydia knew she wasn't going to forget a single second of her interaction with Wick.

"The bullfighters are there for the riders after they dismount or are dismounted. They distract the bulls so the riders can get out of the arena safely."

"Who protects the bullfighters from the bulls?"

Wick smiled again. He didn't make her feel like she was asking stupid questions. He seemed genuinely delighted by her interest in what he did for a living.

"They protect each other."

The hand that he'd had in her hair came to rest on the other side of her hip. Then both of his hands encircled her waist, coming to rest at the small of her back. They were in a real embrace now.

Wick made no move to kiss her. He didn't tug her closer until his body pressed into hers. He simply stood there, holding her as though this was what they had been doing for years.

Lydia could find no reason to protest.

"I didn't know that," she said. "I guess you can tell there's a lot I don't know about what you do. But I want to learn."

"So you can write it all down in your book and decorate it with washi."

"It's called a bujo—my journal." She opened the journal to the page that was still blank and pointed to the not-quite empty space. "It's called a bullet journal. See the dots?"

Wick bowed his head to peer closer. If he turned his head slightly, his lips would press against hers. His gaze lifted, but his head didn't move.

His smile was slow. It didn't spread across his face. He looked amused and slightly terrified. It was the same way her father had always looked at her mother. It was the way Carlos looked at Jane. It was the way Darcy looked at Eliza—that is, when he didn't think anyone was watching.

Wick had said he didn't believe in love. But his gaze was telling Lydia something different. It was telling her that she might be different. Isn't that what every girl wanted? For a guy to think she was different. That she was special. That's how he was looking at her.

This was it. Lydia hadn't believed it would happen to her. But she was standing in the moment where the reality of it was going down. A guy was totally falling for her.

"Are you going to kiss me, Mr. Wickham?" Lydia spoke softly in the dark. Not that anyone was around to hear her. But the moment felt sacred, holy even.

"Yes," he whispered back. "Yes, I am."

His thumb rubbed back and forth across her low back in a windshield-wiping motion. His chest pressed against hers, so much so that she could feel his heart beating in time with hers. His gaze was on her mouth, but he didn't descend to capture her lips.

"Well?" she asked.

"Well, what?"

"Are you going to kiss me or not?"

"I said I would."

And then he stepped away from her. If he hadn't kept hold of her hand, Lydia would've stumbled. Wick tucked her into his side and walked with her away from the pen.

Lydia was so rattled from having been in a haze of desire and then yanked back down to earth that she was silent for a time.

"You know what I think?" she said after a time. "I think you're a player."

They were walking away from the light posts along the drive, so she couldn't see his features, but she sensed a change in him. A stiffening.

"But I don't think that's the full story," she continued.

Wick turned to her. She saw the whites of his eyes, but she still couldn't read his expression. Some of the stiffness left his body as he walked on in silence.

"One thing I've learned is that there's always a kernel of truth to gossip. But there's almost always more to the story." She leaned into him. "Tell me."

"You want me to tell you all my secrets?"

"I do."

"Well, I won't. I'm still trying to impress you."

She laughed. When she did, the corners of Wick's eyes widened as he watched her. His smile was back in place. He pulled her more firmly to his side as they walked on.

"I used to work here," he said, looking up at the manor.

"When I was younger. Mr. Darcy, the elder Mr. Darcy, hired me because he'd seen me in a junior rodeo show. He wanted to sponsor my training."

"How come we never met?"

"I wasn't here for very long."

He let the story drop there. Lydia had known everyone in town. But she didn't remember seeing him at school. Perhaps he was older than her.

"There's more to that story," Lydia guessed.

"Maybe. But it'll cost you."

"What?" Lydia tilted up her head, hoping he'd demand a kiss.

"It'll cost you your story."

"Me?" She pressed her hand to her chest. She was supposed to be interviewing him. But he wanted to know about her. "My dad is great. He's not always the most attentive."

"Let me guess, he's a workaholic."

"Not really. At least not anymore. My sister pretty much runs the family business these days. After my mom died, my dad just wasn't there. So I know what you mean about love having the power to destroy you, even if you're still alive."

They were silent for a few moments longer. Lydia had planned for a light and fun piece on the social life of a bull rider. Instead, she was getting much more of a family drama.

"Any way, I want to be a respected writer. I'm not interested in the family business. I want to make my own way."

"You want to work?"

Lydia was amused at the surprise in his voice. "Who really wants to work? Don't we all want to be taken care of by someone?"

Wick didn't respond. He simply gazed down at her. There was no judgment on his face. Lydia decided that was what she liked most about him.

"What I want," she continued, "is to be respected for something I can do, and I can do well."

"I believe you'll do it."

Lydia's heart did a flip. She managed to stop herself from pounding her fist against her chest to get the organ to behave. She would not let it fall. She couldn't fall for this guy. He was the story.

On the other hand, why couldn't she do both? She could do a glowing exposé on him, showing him in the best light. That would certainly make him fall even harder for her than she was falling for him. He was clearly already halfway there.

CHAPTER SIX

She was already halfway in love with him. That was the thought going through Wick's mind as he gazed down at his little flame.

She was truly beautiful. And easy to talk to. He'd never had this much conversation with a woman. At least not while they were upright and fully clothed.

This was not going to be a bad gig seducing her. Maybe he could even stick around for a while. He couldn't see a reason why not.

Emma was funny. That smile of hers was like sunshine during a storm. And the feel of her in his arms reminded him of a warm blanket on a winter's night. Even though she was young, she was the most down-to-earth woman he'd ever met. Very unlike the women of his past—especially the rich ones who thought the world revolved around them.

Wick could spend the rest of the night listening to her talk about decorative tape and dotted paper and colorful pens. Looking up, he saw that it was well into the night. The moon was high in the sky, and the stars were out. It was late, but he wasn't ready to part from her company.

"Can I show you my favorite place?"

That delighted smile spread across her face. It made his chest tighten. For a moment, he simply stood and stared into those green eyes. They were brighter than the moon, brighter than the sun. Which is likely why he hadn't realized that time had gotten away from him.

His arm was around her waist. It had been there for most of their time together. It hadn't even been a conscious decision on his part. She'd been standing near, and it made perfect sense for her to be nearer to him.

He reached for her hand now. When her fingertips brushed his palm, that tightening in his chest warmed. Oh, she definitely was a flame.

His hand curled around hers, their fingers finding the edges and grooves like puzzle pieces sliding in place. Their knuckles knocked, and their fingers clasped all the way down to the webbing. When they did, Wick heard an audible click.

She felt good at his side. Like she belonged there. Like she should have always been there.

They said nothing as they walked across the land. Wick still knew this place like the back of his hand, even though he hadn't been here in ten years. But he didn't want to think about the events surrounding his eighteenth birthday and after the party, where it all went wrong.

Darcy had done a lot of improvements in that time. Many Wick wouldn't have necessarily made. It looked like they were feeding horses specialized feed instead of allowing them to graze the land. As an athlete, Wick only put whole foods into his body. None of that boxed or synthetic stuff. But it was none of his business.

"Ouch."

"You okay?" Emma asked as she brought her free arm up to rest against his chest.

Wick quickly fixed his features and straightened. "Stubbed my toe on a rock."

He ushered her onward, making sure to face forward so that she wouldn't see the wince of pain that skated across his features. His knee was bothering him again. The nagging wasn't so bad, especially not as he held Emma's hand. Her youth and vitality must be infusing him.

He really wasn't so much older than her. Just eight years if her twenty-first birthday was coming up soon. With them both being in their twenties, it wouldn't be taboo. He'd been pursued by women twice, and a few times thrice his age many times in his life.

There was an innocence to Emma. One that he wanted to keep wrapped up and held close. It wasn't her that he wanted to take advantage of. It was her father's money that Wick wanted to take. Aside from that, he planned to keep Emma at his side for a long time.

"Are you taking me in there to have your wicked way with me, Wick?"

They stood in front of one of the old barns at the edge of the property. It wasn't run-down, but it clearly hadn't been included in Darcy's upgrade project. Paint was peeling from the exterior. The door groaned when Wick pulled it open. The musty smell was more stale than obnoxious.

"This was my hiding place when I lived here. I want to show it to you."

Her smile softened at that. There went that thing in his heart again. His chest was still warm, but at least it wasn't skipping beats again like he was an untried adolescent.

Wick tightened his hold on Emma as he closed the door behind them. There was no lock to keep prying eyes out. He had no plans to seduce her. He just had the urge to show her this part of himself. To see what she thought of it.

She stepped into him, telling him to proceed without words.

He didn't proceed. He stared down at her. They were standing chest to chest again, like the time a few minutes ago when she'd given him the green light to kiss her. The thing was, Wick felt no reason to move into the fast lane. She was a Sunday morning drive down a country road. He was in no rush to get to the final destination.

The thought of the destination had him nearly changing his mind. He could end up wrapping her up in his arms and kissing her. He wanted to. He wanted to taste those cherry red lips. To have those green eyes go hooded with desire. He wanted to wrap that red hair around his fist and tug her head back so he could get the perfect angle for a deep, soul-stealing kiss.

The problem was Wick wasn't sure whose soul was about to get stolen in that moment.

He cleared his throat and turned from her. But still, he did not let go of her hand. Stopping in front of a ladder, he made a nod for her to climb up.

"So you can look at my behind?" she asked indignantly.

"I promise, I won't look."

"I have your word as a gentleman?"

"No, Flame. I'm no gentleman."

She seemed satisfied by that answer and grabbed the first rung to start her climb.

Wick, of course, looked.

He looked because he could. He looked because he wanted to. He wanted to get a sneak peek of the last behind that he would ogle. Because he knew…

He knew she was the one that could solve all of his problems. Including the ones he hadn't had any plans to solve. George Wickham was going to spend the rest of his life with this heiress. Her money would solve his financial problems.

That smile of hers just might solve his lack of a heart problem. He would move heaven and earth to keep her happy.

"I wanted to show you this," he said once he'd come up behind her.

Her green gaze was even wider as she tilted her head back. Her pretty mouth rounded in an O. Her hands clasped together in front of her heart in delight.

"Oh, Wick," she sighed.

It was a struggle to shift his gaze from the wonder of her face to looking up at the wonder spread out above them. Finally, he managed to break his stare. He tilted his head back and looked up through the skylight with her. Stretched out across the night sky was the perfect view of all the stars.

Emma reached her fingers up for them. Wick ran his fingertips up her forearm until their fingers were clasped. Together, they both reached for the stars. He was fool enough to believe they just might touch them.

"Do you bring all the girls up here?" she asked.

"I've never brought anyone up here."

"Why should I believe that?"

"I haven't lied to you. Which is uncharacteristic of me. I always lie to the women I want to seduce."

"And you haven't lied to me?"

"Not once."

"Because you don't want to seduce me?"

"No, I'm not going to seduce you." He brushed a tendril of her red hair from her face. "I'm going to make you fall for me. There's a difference. Seduction is only temporary. I have no plans to let you go."

"Are you gonna kiss me now?"

"Not yet."

"When?"

"Later." Wick gave her a tug, bringing them both down to the ground. "I'm not in a rush."

Emma snuggled into the crook of his arm as they looked up at the stars. She rested a hand over his heart. Wick could've sworn he felt the organ shift inside his chest to beat against her palm.

Soon, he heard the sound of her even breathing. What told him she'd fallen asleep was the gentle snore. Even that delighted him.

He'd never snuggled a woman before. Wick pulled her closer. With Emma locked securely against him, and being totally into him, he relaxed and gazed up at the stars.

Peace settled over him in the knowledge that everything was going to turn out right for him. With that thought, he fell asleep. Pretty soon sleeping turned into dreaming.

dreamed. When she slept, she saw nothing but the
darkness of her eyelids, and her mind went blank.
That was one of the reasons she spent her waking hours in
search of stories to entertain herself.

She hadn't dreamed last night either. Not anything coher-
ent. But this time, when she'd closed her eyes and drifted off
to sleep, she'd seen pinpricks of starlight on the other side of
her eyelids. This time, when she'd closed her eyes and given
her mind over to the dark, she'd felt surrounded by a bright
warmth.

Even with the vision of starlight and the feel of heat, her
mind had known peace. However, her body had remained
aware. Lydia had known she was being held, and she'd never
felt so safe before.

She'd often snuggled into bed with her parents, fitting
herself right between her mom and dad, but always turning
to snuggle into her mother's chest. After her mom passed,
she'd climbed into bed with her oldest sister, Jane, to receive

those snuggles. Lydia had learned quickly that Eliza was both a kicker and a blanket stealer.

She was snuggled up now. But this wasn't Jane's gentle hold. It wasn't Eliza's tough love. Lydia was wrapped up against a firm chest and cradled inside strong arms.

Wick.

Just the thought of his name brought a flush to her face. A flush which spread down her body as her awareness sharpened. Lydia realized she wasn't dreaming. This was real.

Opening her eyes, Lydia saw that, from her head to her toes, her body was in contact with his. One of her legs was thrown over his muscled thighs. An arm was slung over his chest, her hand resting against his beating heart. Her head was tucked into the crook of his neck. She felt his chin resting against the top of her head.

She'd never been held like this. Certainly not by her mother or sisters. Definitely not by a guy.

She'd never gone past kissing and a little heavy petting with the guys she'd dated. She hadn't done either of those things with Wick, yet this was the most intimate she'd ever been with a man.

Most guys she'd dated hadn't been able to keep their eyes on her. Not when Emma was around. Eventually, she'd realized each guy had only asked her out or tried to get close to her as a way to get in with Emma. Either because of her money, or because of her looks, or just because she was, well, Emma.

Wick had looked at Emma earlier this evening. But only for a second. Now he was here with her, and he hadn't brought her up even once. He was here for her.

And he was awake.

Wick ran his fingers up and down her forearms in a lazy motion. He didn't jostle her, trying to make her stir. He wasn't pushing her away. In fact, his other arm was looped over her torso, where he rubbed his thumb in lazy circles against her hip.

"Am I still dreaming?" she asked.

"You're awake," he said, continuing his circular caresses. "Having what you want when you're awake is even better than dreaming."

Lydia loved the way his voice rumbled through her. It was like a blanket wrapping her up on a cool autumn morning. It was balmy in the barn this morning. What surprised her most was the fact that it was a new day. She couldn't believe she'd spent the night with a man.

"My family is going to flip out that I didn't come home last night."

She said the words, but she still made no move to get up and leave. She did lift up on her elbows to gaze down at Wick. It was a mistake.

When they'd first met, it was under the harsh, unflattering glow of fluorescent lights in the Pemberley ballroom. Last night, most of the time, his face had been clouded in shadows. A few twinkles of starlight had given her glimpses into his dark eyes. Now he had the full force of the sun on him, and he was even more attractive in the morning light.

There was a light stubble on his jaw. His hair was mussed. His gaze was relaxed.

"You're a grown woman."

"Yeah, but it's still irresponsible to spend the night out with a man I just met."

Wick tightened the hold he had on Lydia's hip. "Does it really feel like we just met?"

Lydia tugged her bottom lip into her mouth. Wick tracked the motion. He reached up with his thumb and traced the curve of her mouth.

"You know more about me than... anyone." His thumb

slacked down to rest beneath her chin as his gaze went far away.

"I wish I could say the same. But the person who knows the most about me is my best friend..."

Lydia trailed off. She wanted to bring Wick's attention back to her, not turn it to Emma. Finally, she had a guy who wanted her for her, and not because he was trying to use her as a stepping stone to someone else.

"The friend you were with at the pageant?" he asked.

Lydia couldn't hide her wince. She dipped her head and scrubbed her hand over her face in an attempt to wipe off the look.

"Or maybe she's not your friend? What is it you girls call it these days? Your frenemy."

"No, she's not my frenemy. She's the best, and I love her to bits. It's just... It's just that guys are usually into her and completely look past me."

Wick was quiet for a long moment. So long that Lydia was uncertain if he was paying attention to her. She chanced a glance up and caught him staring at her in amazement. He didn't speak until he'd held her gaze for a full ten seconds.

"My friend Denny pointed the two of you out to me. I barely glanced at her. All I could think was I wanted to meet you, figure out a way to get close to you."

"Really?"

Wick waved an arm around the open air. "Here we are."

Yes, here they were, alone in a barn after falling asleep in each other's arms. Emma was nowhere to be found. She would be thrilled when Lydia told her about the new guy she was dating. That is if...

"Wick?"

"Yeah, Flame?"

"Do you want to see me again?"

"I don't want to stop seeing you right now." The whites of

his teeth flashed at her, making her feel like she'd been stalked, caught, and devoured by something much larger than herself. "Can I kiss you?"

"Finally!" Lydia tilted her chin up to receive his kiss. At the last moment, she jerked her head back down and fluttered her lashes at him. "Is that all you want to do?"

"Oh, my red flame," Wick chuckled, capturing her chin between his thumb and forefinger again. "The things I dreamed about doing to you..."

"You can, you know. I want to. I don't want to wait. Not with you."

His gaze softened, as did his hold on her. Lydia wished she could take it all back. Her sisters told her men didn't like women to be too forward. All the self-help and manifesting books she read told her that she had to ask for exactly what she wanted.

Well, Lydia wanted Wick. Not just for today. For the rest of her life. He was going to be her one and only. She felt certain of that with every fiber of her being.

"No, Flame. I'm not going to do those things with you."

"You don't want me?"

"I want you more than anything in the world."

His dark eyes were so bright, so open. Looking into them, Lydia saw the truth of his words. She also felt like he didn't let anyone else see so deeply into him.

"I'm not the kind of man to take a girl's innocence in a barn." He planted a tender kiss on her nose. "Definitely not your innocence." His next kiss was at the corner of her right eye. "You deserve satin sheets and candles and a bed of roses." He dipped his head to kiss the cone of her ear.

"I'd like that."

"Good, because that's what you're going to get."

"When?"

"When you realize we're perfect together."

"I can already see that."

Again, he flashed her those white teeth. Lydia tilted her head to the side, exposing her neck like an obedient wolf would do to her Alpha. Except they were the only two in this pack.

"I have a feeling," Wick said, his bottom lip brushing her top lip, "that when the two of us finally come together, the earth will move."

He canted his head to line his lips with hers. Beneath them came a rumbling sound. Like a pack of rabid wolves pounding their paws up the stairs. When both Wick and Lydia lifted their heads to seek out the oncoming danger, there only stood a man at the top of the stairs.

Fitz Darcy.

CHAPTER EIGHT

This was why Wick didn't care to dream. Anytime he opened himself up to want, someone came along to snatch it from him. Or, worse, to pull dark clouds over his head that would turn the dream into a nightmare.

Wick rose, using his body to shield Emma from the unwelcome intruder. Of course, he knew that they were the two that were trespassing on Darcy's land. But still, the guy had eyes. Clearly, he could see he'd walked in on a scenario where he was most unwelcome.

The two men eyed each other warily. The only hint Darcy gave that he acknowledged Wick's presence was in the lift of his aristocratic chin. Even as a young man, Darcy would always lift his chin whenever he encountered Wick. Though the two were the same age, Wick had always stood a few inches over him. That chin flick was Darcy's way of still letting Wick know that, as the help, he was beneath him no matter how tall either of them stood.

This was the last thing Wick needed. It was the last thing he wanted. Wick had known he would have to come face to face with Darcy at some point with his return to Austen

Valley. Of course, this unwanted reunion would happen when Wick was in a vulnerable moment.

He'd lost himself in that almost kiss with Emma. He hadn't even tasted those delectable lips properly, and he'd been a goner. Just the hint of the sweetness had clouded his mind and begun to strip away his good sense.

Truth be told, Wick had been about ready to take her up on her offer to do more. Though, no, he doubted he would have. It was clear that the girl was an innocent.

Clear by the way her breath caught when he'd simply brushed his lower lip against hers. In fact, he wondered if she'd ever been kissed. She certainly hadn't been kissed properly. Which was another reason why Wick would wait.

He wanted everything done properly and thoroughly with her. He wanted everything she did with her innocence to only be done with him. He'd be her one and only from this moment out. He just needed to get past this moment of the chin raising, interrupting, prideful man with eyes filled with a prejudice toward him.

Looking at Darcy looking at her, Wick got an irrational sense of cave man. He wanted to sling Emma over his shoulder and shout *mine*. But when he opened his mouth, it was Emma's voice that came out in a shrill shout of indignation.

"Jeez, Fitz, do you knock?" she said.

Darcy's chin dipped as he canted his head to look past Wick. His brows lifted, and his hand went to his chest. "I beg your pardon," he said in that stiff formal way of his. "But this is my property."

Behind him, Wick felt more than heard Emma rise from their lover's nest. It seemed the woman was prepared to fight his battles for him. For a brief second, Wick's entire body filled with warmth. Once upon a time, that had been an impossible feat with all the ice he'd purposefully packed into himself so that he'd feel nothing. But in the space of a night, she'd thawed him entirely.

Wick stepped forward before she could say anymore. When he came face to face with his nemesis, he was gratified to know that he still maintained that inch on the man.

Darcy raised that chin. High enough to almost negate Wick's advantage. Wick had the urge to go up onto his tiptoes, but the injury in his knee threatened to buckle if he gave into the pettiness of the standoff.

"George," said Darcy.

"Fitz," said Wickham.

"Wasn't aware I extended an invitation to you to come back here."

"I'm with the rodeo."

"I know." Fitz raised an imperial brow. "I'm aware you're a rider. The pens are set up on the other side of the property. What I'm sure I didn't do was to invite you into this barn, or any other part of my private property."

Darcy sniffed as he said that last bit—*my property*. Wick had been welcomed here while the elder Mr. Darcy was alive. If the old man had been here when the incident had gone down, he was certain the man would've believed him. Or at least deigned to hear Wick out.

Not the younger Darcy. He'd thrown Wick out on his backside, despite Wick's pleas to explain.

"You might mount things for a living now," Darcy said, "but I'll thank you not to trifle with innocents in my barn."

Once again, Darcy's gaze flicked past Wick to Emma. But the fiery redhead wasn't where Wick had left her. She'd come up to stand at his back.

"He wasn't trifling with me," she said. "Nothing happened. Unfortunately. It was about to before we were so rudely—"

"Your family is looking for you," Darcy interrupted her. "I

can do you the favor of being discreet and not telling them who you were in here with."

The blow struck Wick low. This man had always had the ability to make him feel like he had a dirty hand outstretched in need. It was the way of rich people. The way of most of the wealthy… except the woman standing beside him.

"I don't need you to tell anybody anything," she said. "I'm going to tell my family exactly where I was and who I was with."

"I don't think they'll take kindly to knowing you were with a man such as him." Darcy chucked a thumb at Wick.

"Clearly you don't know him the way I do," Emma said, coming to stand in front of Wick as though she were a bull fighter. "George Wickham is a perfect gentleman, I'll have you know. He didn't take a single advantage with me, even though every advantage was offered to him."

Wick glanced down at her. If he believed in love, he would call this feeling falling into it. When Emma laced her fingers through his and pressed into his side, that sealed the deal. He was never letting her go.

"I don't know what game you're playing, Wickham," Darcy was saying. "But her family will not play along. Trust me on that one. Best you just leave her be."

With those words, Emma's fingers went slack around his. Darcy's words had hurt her. Wick wanted to lash out and punch the arrogant piece of work in his nose. But to do that, he'd have to let her go. That was something he was not prepared to do.

"Don't listen to him." Wick turned his back on Darcy. "Even if your family will disapprove, the only opinion I care about is yours. If you'll have me, I'm never leaving your side."

She lifted her head then. Those fiery red curls bounced into her eyes. Wick brushed them away with their joined hands so he could peer into her green depths and show her the truth.

"I'm awake now," he continued. "The dream's too good to go back to sleep."

With those words, the smile came back on her face, and he felt like he was the king of the world.

"You can't mean to marry her," said Darcy. "She's a child."

"She's not a child," said Wick, still giving the man his back.

"I'm not a child," said Emma at the same time, but she peered over Wick's shoulder to glare at Darcy. "I'm twenty-one, legal and full-grown."

Wick knew she was only twenty. That her birthday was just weeks away. It was close enough.

"He's not the marrying type," said Darcy, his attention on Emma. "Trust me. My family has experience with it—my sister in particular."

The harsh breath that blew from Wick's nostrils rivaled that of a bull champing at the bit to get out of the chute. Ten years and the accusation still hurt. No one had believed Wick. Everyone had believed Georgiana. She'd been coddled while he'd been kicked out and left to fend for himself.

"I trust him," Emma said as she wrapped her arms around his waist. She looked up into his eyes. Her gaze was wide and trusting.

She wasn't the first woman to ever look at Wick like that. She was the first woman whose trust Wick wanted to hold close to his chest.

"I am going to marry you," said Wickham. The words escaped his mouth before his brain had a chance to process them. In the aftermath of the matrimonial revelations, he realized he didn't want to take it back. He only needed to add a caveat. "One day."

"Why wait?" she asked.

It was a fair question. One Wick couldn't think up a single answer for. He'd made up his mind about her. And it looked like she'd made up her mind about him.

He'd thought they'd been traveling in the slow lane for the last twelve hours. What he'd missed was the sign for the speed limit. They'd broken it somewhere between hello in the first moments they'd met.

CHAPTER NINE

*E*verything looked brighter this morning. Well, once that dark cloud made its way across the sky. And then the smaller gray ones followed slowly in its wake. Then the sun broke through, and everything was bright.

Lydia tilted her head up to take in some of the warm sunshine and promptly coughed. The new dark cloud was coming from beneath the hood of Wick's vintage Ford Mustang. There might be a little trouble under the hood, but for all outward appearances, the classic car was well kept inside and out.

After a few moments of tinkering, the engine came to life with a roar. Wick slammed the hood closed. He cast Lydia what should've been called a sheepish grin, but then he flashed those sharp incisors, revealing the wolf that he was. Lydia squirmed in her seat, perfectly content to be the sheep caught in this man's clutches.

Wick reached for her hand across the console. Lydia slid her fingers into his, just as easily as she'd slipped into the car seat, just as easily as she'd followed him into the barn and fallen asleep in his arms. She was exactly where she was supposed to be.

She ignored the spring in the leather seat biting into her hip. Instead, she looked out at the scenery of the valley she'd lived in all her life. The trees she'd seen every day on her ride to school looked greener. Flowers of every color sprang up alongside the road. A flock of birds trailed behind them as Wick drove leisurely on the country lane in his sports car.

His profile was heart-stoppingly handsome and already so dear to her. With their entwined hands, Lydia reached up and brushed her fingertips across his temple. He smiled at the gesture, turning his head and pressing a kiss to the side of her index finger.

"Are you hungry?" he asked.

"I couldn't eat. I'm too nervous."

"Nervous?"

"We're about to go and tell my family we're engaged. So yeah, I'm nervous. My stomach is in knots."

Something in his jawline changed. His chin went up a little higher. His nostrils flared slightly. His gaze was still on the road, but his lashes lowered even though the sun wasn't directly in his eyesight.

"Are you having second thoughts, Flame?"

"About us?" Lydia brushed her thumb over his bottom lip. "Not even slightly."

Wick turned to her. The relief on his face was evident in the widening of his eyes and the relaxation of his mouth. He pressed another kiss to her fingers before turning his attention back to the road.

"It's my family I'm worried about," Lydia clarified.

"Worried they won't approve of me?"

"I'm worried you won't approve of them. They're… a lot."

Wick let out a huff of air. It sounded part laugh, part… something else. She didn't get a chance to question it. Her mind went fuzzy as he pressed more kisses to her fingertip and into her palm.

She had a moment of irrational jealousy at her hand. Their lips had only barely touched back in the barn before being so rudely interrupted by Fitz Darcy. True, she and Wick had been trespassing. And sure, Darcy had come searching for her out of concern. But his concern had cost Lydia what she knew would have been a soul-stealing kiss. Likely more.

"You know," she said, turning in the passenger seat to face him, "that turn-off over there is a popular parking spot in this town."

Wick chuckled again. Lydia would never get tired of the sound and the feel and the texture of his laughter.

"We can make out later," he said. "We can make out for the rest of our lives. I need to apologize to your father first for having you out late and making him worry."

Lydia doubted her father had noticed her absence. John Bennett rarely noticed much these days. His mind had been in a perpetual fog since his wife had died ten years ago. It was her sisters who Wick should worry about.

"Are we really doing this?" asked Lydia.

"Getting married, you mean?"

Lydia nodded.

"We can go to the chapel right now." Wick pressed a kiss to her wrist. Her pulse jumped at his caress. "But I'm sure you want some grand society wedding so it can be in the papers."

"No, I don't want that at all," said Lydia. "I like to write the gossip stories. I don't want to be the object of the gossip."

"You don't want our story in the papers?"

Lydia's chest tightened. She was supposed to be writing his story. She was supposed to be finding something gossip-worthy to write about him. So far, the most salacious thing about George Wickham was his relationship with her.

"We can wait," he said.

She must have been sitting there silent for a while. When she blinked, she noted that they'd long passed Lover's Lane and were nearing the turn-off to her family's ranch. The tension had returned to Wick's jawline, and his eyelids were lowered to half-mast.

"Wait?" she asked.

"To get married."

Her chest tightened again, but it twisted in the other way.

"I won't change my mind about you," he continued. "I'm sure this is what I want. You're what I want. I'm going to make you a very happy woman, Flame. I'm also going to do very wicked things with that mouth of yours once we're married."

"Really?" Lydia's grin was so wide it hurt her face. "Then we definitely shouldn't wait."

"That's my girl." He pressed another kiss to her hand. Then he trailed kisses from her palm to her wrist, then back up to her fourth finger where a ring would soon rest.

Lydia waited for the panic to settle in. For the doubt to flutter in her mind. It never came. Doubt about his intentions with her didn't make an appearance. She'd fallen for George Wickham at first sight.

But something else niggled at the back of her mind.

Lydia knew she should keep her mouth shut. She didn't want to ruin the moment. Her curiosity and need for gossip got the better of her.

"Can I ask you about her?"

Wick's last kiss against her ring finger turned into a sigh. His gaze was hooded once more when he looked over at her. His jaw tensed slightly, but Lydia could feel it wasn't as rock hard as it looked.

"Did you know her?" he asked.

Neither of them needed to clarify whom they were referring to.

Lydia shook her head. Georgiana Darcy was the same age as her, but she hadn't gone to public school. She hadn't done any of the social things kids her age did. She'd been kept away like a protected piece of china no one was allowed to play with.

"I was the hired help. She was the coddled heiress." He winced then. The words had been flowing freely. He pursed his lips together before moving on. "I never led her on. But I'm no saint. I earned my reputation with other women."

Lydia didn't care to know about the other women. Just the one who made his jaw tense whenever she was mentioned. "What happened?"

"It was my eighteenth birthday. The staff had thrown a little party for me. Nothing fancy. Mr. Darcy had passed by then. But for a birthday present, he'd left me a two-year scholarship to a state school for my Associates in Animal Science."

"That was very generous."

"It was." Wick sighed, his head bobbing forward as though the weight of the world were on his shoulder. "Later that night, after the party, when I went to my bedroom, Georgiana was there."

"Oh, no. I can imagine what happened next."

"You can?" His head jerked to her in surprise.

"She made a pass at you. You tried to let her down. But not before the two of you were discovered."

Wick's mouth hung open, flapping like a fish out of water. Slowly, it stretched into a shallow grin that was full of wonder as he gazed at her like she was the shining light of truth. He slowed the car down, then he reached for her.

Before the car came to a complete halt, the engine backfired, causing them to jump apart. Once again, Lydia coughed as a plume of smoke billowed up from under the hood.

"Been meaning to get that fixed," he said.

"It's fine. We're here. It's this turn."

Wick glanced over, and his brows rose at the sight of the Bennett ranch. "This is where you live?"

CHAPTER TEN

ick coughed at the dirt his tires kicked up as they made their way down the winding road. They had only traveled a couple of miles over from Pemberley. He remembered that there was a family that lived here. He couldn't recall their surnames. He hadn't spent much time off the Pemberley ranch when he'd lived here for those few years before he was kicked off the ranch.

The Pemberley estate was vast. So, too, was Rosing's Ranch, where the slightly less rich wing of the Darcy family made their home. Wick had seen the small ranch tucked in between the two massive estates, but he'd never had a reason to visit. He couldn't remember if the family had been called the Woodhouses. But he supposed so.

Amazing. The woman of his dreams had been just a few acres away, within horse riding distance, and he hadn't known it. Just another thing Darcy had taken from him with no true cause besides his own haughty prejudice and wounded pride.

Wick would have expected a much bigger house for the

Woodhouses than the single-story manor he saw. The home was a sprawling ranch style. The roof looked like it was due for an update soon. There was paint chipping off one of the dormers. There was an old beat-up pickup truck in the drive, not any of the new line of Fords that were parked in Darcy's garage. The fencing could use some mending, but wasn't that the case of all ranches and farms?

Still, it looked cozy. Lived in. Nothing like what he'd expect a millionaire heiress and her family would inhabit. Maybe this was their summer cottage?

"This is it," she said. "Home sweet home."

"This is your only home?"

"Yeah." She snorted. "Unless you count the place in the back for the horse trainer."

Wick nodded. He didn't make a move to get out of the car. Instead, he leaned against his steering wheel and continued to take it all in. Something seemed… off.

"Have you lived here your whole life?"

"I was born in my parents' bedroom. I didn't give my mom enough time to make it to the hospital."

She was grinning. For a second, his confusion left him, and he was blinded by the green light in her eyes. Gah, the way she looked at him, with complete trust and admiration. No one had ever looked at him like that before.

Wick got the sudden urge to shift into reverse, turn the car around, and run away with her. To outrun the weight of his past and the debt that refused to let him go. To bypass the present where he'd need to convince her family that he was worthy of her.

Because, truth be told, he was not. He never would be. As soon as they got out of the car, she would find out.

His booted toe tapped the gas lightly. As the engine revved, he realized he couldn't outrun any of it. As though to confirm his thoughts, the car backfired.

In the distance, Wick heard a horse cry out in fear. The sound was coupled by the hoarse shout of a man. Wick looked up in time to see the horse rear and an elderly man go down.

"No!" Emma shouted.

The old man had had the horse's reins in his hands. When the horse reared, the man hadn't let go. He had been looking in the distance at Wick and Emma's arrival. He let go of the reins too late, and with his loss of control of the rearing horse, he also lost his balance and was falling to the ground. The spooked horse's hooves were high in the air. When the animal landed, there was a good chance its weight would come crashing down on the old man.

Wick was out of the car in the blink of an eye. He ignored the protest of his leg and rushed to the fence where the man and horse were penned in. Leaping over the structure, Wick came down hard on his injured leg. He didn't have time to focus on the pain. The horse was rearing up again.

The animal had missed the old man lying on the ground the first time. But with Wick running up and hopping the fence, it startled the beast once more.

It was an amateur move. But it was done in the heat of the moment. He'd also acted on the heels of Emma leaping out of the car a beat behind him.

Wick took a deep breath, infusing his whole body with calm despite the rapid beat of his heart and the throb in his leg. He moved slowly toward the nervous horse, his hands down and his head slightly bowed.

"Calm down there, bud," he said in a gentle tone that belied his need to shout the command. "It was just a bit of noise. That's it."

The horse blinked his big, brown eyes. His ears, which had been tipped forward and visibly stiff, began to relax and flatten. The animal took a couple of steps back and away from the prone man.

It had been a while since Wick had dealt with a creature that was gentle by nature. On the back of a bull that did not want him there, he had to show brute force to keep his seat. Horses weren't aggressive beasts by nature. Truth be told, neither were bulls. But each animal was living proof that it reflected the treatment of the humans around it.

The horse lowered his head and sighed through his nostrils. Wick reached out and ran a hand down its long neck, giving it a scratch behind the ear.

With the horse under control, Wick turned his attention to the fallen man. Emma was already at his side. She was on the ground, her dress covered in dirt as she knelt over him. But she didn't seem to care.

"Are you okay, Dad?"

Dad? What was Mr. Woodhouse doing out here tending to his own horses? Even Darcy had ranch hands helping him over at Pemberley.

Wick wrapped the horse's lead around a post, then he headed over to Emma and her father. He reached a hand to the older man to help him up. Mr. Woodhouse squinted his eyes, taking a moment to take Wick in.

The moment felt rife to Wick. The thing he hated most in the world was to be scrutinized by anyone wealthy. To have them cast their judgment on him and his wallet and find him wanting.

"I owe you my thanks." Mr. Woodhouse took the offered hand and allowed Wick to lend him his strength to bring him upright. "Lefroy is usually a good stallion. But he doesn't take to loud noises. It's usually quiet here in the morning."

"I'm sorry about that, sir. I've been meaning to get that issue with my car fixed."

"Sounds like your engine is running rich."

Wick frowned. He'd thought it was the distributor cap. Thinking about the other man's diagnosis, Wick wondered if he could be right. Mr. Woodhouse's words made his brows rise. "You know your way around cars, sir?"

"You know horses, son?"

A grin spread over Wick's face unbidden. It was only there for a fleeting second. The next words out of his mouth would change any good estimation Mr. Woodhouse was forming of him. "I'm in the rodeo, sir."

"George is a bull rider, Dad," said Emma. "One of the best."

"Is that where you've been all night? Out at the rodeo? With a bull rider?"

Her cheeks flamed the same color as her hair.

"It's my fault," said Wick. "We lost track of the time."

Mr. Woodhouse examined him. Wick held still for the perusal. He waited for the man to lift his chin and sneer down at him. He waited for those pale eyes, slightly less vibrant than his daughter's, to look at him with disdain. He waited for the set down to pass the older man's lips.

None of that happened.

Instead, the old man bobbed his head in a nod of acceptance. His mouth compressed into a thin line that could be interpreted as consent. There wasn't exactly approval in his green gaze, but it wasn't condemnation.

All told, it amounted to high praise in Wick's estimation. It also made the heavy weight of the last ten years in Wick's chest feel lighter.

"I swear to you that nothing disrespectful happened between me and your daughter, sir."

"No?" Was that disappointment in the older man's tone? Or disbelief?

"I did kiss her," said Wick. "But just barely."

The old man grinned. A quiet chuckle rose from his chest as he regarded Wick.

The chuckle shook loose a memory from Wick's past. Old Mr. Darcy had the same grin. He was a man that never laughed out loud, but he had that same quiet chuckle whenever Wick had done something that impressed him.

"I'm going to marry her."

Wick had no memory of making the conscious decision to allow that declaration to burst from his mouth. Now that the words were out, he couldn't take them back. He didn't want to. He had every intention of marrying Emma Woodhouse. It had gone beyond a financial means to an end. He simply could no longer imagine his life without the lush redhead with the fire in her green gaze at his side.

A glance at Emma told Wick she had"no r'grets about how her fiancé had decided to deliver the news. He reached out a hand to her. She came to him willingly, lovingly. The way she looked at him made him feel like he was the richest man in the world.

Another of those quiet chuckles escaped her father's chest. "Is that so? Are you getting married, Lydia?"

Wick frowned at the name her father called her. Had the fall knocked him on the head? Or perhaps that was her middle name? Or a nickname her family used?

"I was going to introduce you two first," Emma said. "George, this is my father, John Bennett."

Bennett? Were they both in the habit of using their middle names to refer to each other? Emma Lydia Woodhouse and John Bennett Woodhouse?

No, that couldn't be right. Come to think of it, the name Bennett rang a bell in Wick's head. He'd once heard Darcy talking about a Bennett. A red-headed girl who lived next door. Just like his Flame.

"It's good to meet you, son." Mr. Bennett held out his hand. The man's hair was mostly gray… but there were a few fading bits of red at the sides just above his ears.

Wick found himself taking the hand as his head continued to reel with the truth of the situation.

CHAPTER ELEVEN

"You're engaged? Are you crazy?"

"You're engaged? That's delightful."

Though both of her sisters spoke at the same time and over one another, Lydia had no trouble at all discerning whose words were whose.

Jane beamed at her. Her approving smile was just as bright as the diamond on her finger from her fake boyfriend, turned very real boyfriend, and now doting fiancé Carlos Bingley. The two had said they were gonna take it slow and date, but speed was more hare than tortoise in this situation. Carlos had already purchased the manor nearby, and Jane was over each day, measuring the drapes.

Meanwhile, Eliza's cheeks were nearly as red as her hair. She looked like she had when they were kids and she insisted she could hold her breath the longest. She'd once held her breath for two minutes and two seconds while on the playground at school. Her cheeks had been that red. Except right now, her mouth hung open. Her green eyes were huge as they bored into Lydia in incredulity.

It didn't matter. Neither her sisters' praise nor their ire

was going to shake Lydia today. Not when she stood under the radiant glow of true love.

"Jane, Eliza, I'd like to introduce you to your future brother-in-law, George Wickham."

Wick stood beside her. He was a tall and certain presence, despite the baffled look on his face. He ran his hand down his face as he eyed Jane's accepting smile. He raked his fingers through his hair as he winced at Eliza's suspicious glare.

He hadn't said another word since leaving her father outside. Wick opened his mouth, his tongue touching the tip of his teeth as though he was about to speak. Then he shut his mouth and grimaced. He parted his lips again, only to choke on whatever failed to come out.

Lydia snaked an arm through his, lending him her support. They were a unit now. The gesture didn't relax him. If anything, his strong biceps tensed harder than a rock.

"Wait, Wickham?" said Eliza, pointing a finger at his chest. "Don't I know you?"

"I... um..." Wick blinked his eyes rapidly, as though he was having difficulty bringing Eliza into focus.

Eliza stepped closer. "You used to work at Pemberley, didn't you?"

"Ah... I..." The hand that was in his hair scrubbed rapidly at the base of his neck.

"You were old Mr. Darcy's junior rodeo phenom, weren't you?"

"What?" Jane clapped her hands together in delight. "I can't believe we never met before."

Wick cleared his throat. He looked between Eliza and Jane. Once again, he opened his mouth. When nothing came out, he rubbed his hand over his face and down his jaw, pinching his chin between his thumb and forefinger along the way.

Men were often dumbfounded when confronted with one of her sisters. Two left them speechless. All three Bennett girls together had on occasion driven lesser men to tears. Lydia refused to let her sisters intimidate the man she was going to spend the rest of her life with.

"He's only recently returned to Austen Valley," said Lydia. "He's in the rodeo."

"Only recently returned? So how do you two know each other?"

"You're in the rodeo? That sounds so exciting."

"Yes, it is exciting." Lydia preened, choosing to ignore Eliza's question and focus on Jane's. "He's riding this weekend, and we're all going to be in his corner routing for him."

"Oh, absolutely," said Jane.

"How long have you two been dating, Lyddie?" asked Eliza.

Lydia glanced up at Wick. His mouth hung open, but no words came out. When he turned to face her, his gaze was wide and cloudy, as though he was looking at her for the first time.

"We just met last night," Lydia confessed.

Jane's welcoming smile dimmed, like a switch being yanked down to extinguish the light. Eliza flashed her teeth, like a shark circling in deep water.

"Last night?" asked Jane.

Lydia nodded, sliding her hand down Wick's arm to reach his hand. She laced their fingers together. Her fingers were warm. His were ice cold.

"Now you're engaged?" asked Jane. "That is rather sudden."

"You're engaged with Carlos after a week," said Lydia. "It took only a few hours for Wick and me to fall in love."

"Is that all you fell into?" Eliza addressed Wick, her shrewd gaze sending daggers at the man.

Lydia stepped in front of Wick. Though he had a good few inches on her and her sisters, she knew the bull rider was no match for Eliza if she decided he needed to be bucked out of the house.

"You were out all night," said Eliza. "Did he take liberties with you, Lydia?"

"A, that's none of your business. And two, I'm a grown woman."

Both Jane and Eliza rounded on Wickham. All friendliness had dropped from Jane's green eyes, and her gaze was shuttered. Eliza cracked her knuckles and jutted out her chin. Lydia spread out her arms as though she could ward off the eminent attack.

For his part, Wick finally seemed to snap out of whatever daze he'd fall into. He came to attention now that his life was in danger.

"I didn't," he said as Eliza came up on his left. "We didn't," he insisted to Jane as she flanked his right. "We fell *ah*-sleep. We didn't sleep *to-gether*. I didn't take any liberties. She still has them all."

Wick let go of Lydia's hand, dropping it like it was a hot poker and he was a doused flame. He held up both hands in front of his chest as though he were about to be arrested. Which wasn't too far from the truth.

"That's enough out of the two of you," said Lydia as her sisters continued to patrol her fiancé like they were going to produce handcuffs. "We can talk more about this when you two grow up."

Lydia grabbed Wick by the arm and tugged him down the hall and into her room. By the time she got to her bedroom door, she was pulling and dragging more than tugging. Wick had even begun leaning back and trying to plant his heels on the ground to halt the forward motion. By then, they were already crossing the threshold of her bedroom door.

"I should go," he said, staring at the door as though he didn't know where he was.

"Ignore them," Lydia said, closing and locking the door behind her. "They'll come around. Besides, you have my father's blessing."

John Bennett had opened his arms wide after shaking Wick's hand. It might have been a side effect of Wick coming to his aid after spooking Lefroy. It may have been her father's glee that he was coming close to outnumbering his daughters with not one but two more men on the ranch. Or it may have been that, just like with his daughter, her father had seen something special in George Wickham in the short time of their acquaintance.

Wick was looking at her now with something like fire in his eyes. It wasn't the smoldering flame of last night or this morning. It looked more like dark clouds of smoke with patches of gray fog.

"Your name's Lydia?"

"Of course it is," she said, slipping out of her shoes. "Eliza calls me Lyddie sometimes, to remind me that she's older. My best friend Emma does it, too."

"Emma?"

"But when Em says it, it's not a power move." She took off first one and then the other earring, setting them on a nightstand. "It's purely out of affection, so I don't mind so much. I like that you call me Flame."

"Em?"

"Emma Woodhouse. She's my best friend. She's going to flip when she finds out I'm engaged. But then she'll come around and be ready to plan the wedding. She'll be the maid of honor."

"Emma Woodhouse will be the maid of honor?"

"Oh, Wick, you'll love her." Lydia wrinkled her nose. "Maybe. Probably. The two of you don't have much in common. But she'll love you 'cause I love you. And because you love me."

Lydia placed her hands on his chest. She felt the strong beat of his heart under her fingertips. It was racing. So was hers.

"Hey," she said, flattening her palms against his pecs and spreading her fingers to reach more of him. "We're alone now. In my bedroom. With my father's blessing…"

With her right hand, Lydia popped open one button from his shirt. His skin was chilled, but a light sheen of sweat clung to him. She leaned in and pressed a kiss to his flesh, causing his skin to instantly heat.

Then the heat and his bare flesh were gone. Wick took a step away from her. That step was unsteady, and his right leg wobbled when his heel met the floor.

"I think we need to slow down," he said, putting his hands back up in the defensive *Stop in the Name of Love* position. His fingers were trembling this time.

"Yeah," said Lydia, taking measured steps toward him. "Slow is good. Let's go slow."

She reached for him again. This time, her hands snaked around his neck. She tugged him down to her. He came willingly, almost as though he couldn't help himself.

Wick's mouth crashed into hers, not gently. His lips pulled from hers as she yielded to him. Her hands went into his hair. His forearms came around her back, pressing her fully into him. They were lost in each other long before the need to come up for air was a pressing matter.

Once that need hit them and they sprang apart, both were gasping for air. Wick peered down at her with a hazy gaze. There was a spark in his eyes, like a flash of lightning filled with desire. Surrounding that were dark clouds that looked at her as though he were lost.

Lydia reached for him again, aiming to assure him that

she was his safe space. He backed away from her, sidestepping until he was at the door.

"I have to go," he said, re-buttoning his shirt.

"Go?"

"Go where?"

He looked up at her with that lost expression weighing heavily on his brows. "Training. I have to train."

CHAPTER TWELVE

ick sped down the road, away from the manor house. The car only choked and backfired once during the drive down the straight and narrow road. It seemed to understand his need to get out of there, away from the Bennett Ranch.

Bennett.

Lydia.

Lydia Bennett.

The name sounded wrong in his head, but the taste of her on his tongue still filled him. Wick's head might have been clouded, but within that dense fog was a feeling of satiety that had come from kissing that pliable mouth. The feel of those lush, warm curves was still present in his hands. That flaming red hair and those bright green eyes were still vivid in his vision.

She wasn't who he thought she was. Why hadn't she told him? She'd entirely led him to believe that she was Emma Woodhouse, heiress and holder of trusted funds that would save his sorry hide. When, in fact, she was just another rancher's daughter in a crowded house whose roof needed repairing.

The fact that Wick's hands itched to pick up a hammer, the fact that he now knew exactly how much space her bed took up in her room, the fact that he could already see himself in there, with her, made Wick's foot shift from the gas to the brake.

Luckily for him, the car was a manual. There were gears to shift before he could make the fool decision to turn around and go back to her. He needed to put distance between them. He got his feet on board and pressed on the gas pedal.

But his hands still twitched on the steering wheel. His heart was racing. Likely because he'd almost fallen into her trap. He'd almost been ensnared by a young, naïve, gorgeous, grinning, poor, precocious, dazzling, desirable—

The squeal of brakes assaulted his ears. Wick smelled the burning rubber of his tires. His grip on the steering wheel switched, readying to make a U-turn to return to that sweetness he'd found with her.

That singular peace he'd known lying with her beneath the stars.

That bit of heaven he'd woken to when he'd sipped his first taste of her.

And then there was that last kiss. The thought of it had Wick pressing his lips together. When he did, he tasted the saccharine remnants of her in his mouth.

His Flame.

Lydia.

Lydia Bennett the rancher's daughter.

Not Emma the heiress.

Wick straightened his arms at ten and two on the steering wheel. He pressed the pedal to the metal of the floorboards to make a beeline away from the Bennett Ranch for good.

His blood pumped as he broke the speed limit to get farther and farther away from temptation.

Last night had been a dream. A good dream, one he'd remember for the rest of his days. But the rest of his days were limited if he didn't get himself out of the very real nightmare his debt had him drowning in.

When he pulled back onto the grounds of Pemberley, his gaze immediately went to the roof of the estate. The dark gray tiles that made up the sloping structure were immaculate. Wick doubted that more than five people, Darcy and servants included, called the imposing mansion their home. The heiress who had been responsible for Wick's initial demise had been packed away shortly after he had been kicked out. By the time she'd stepped out of finishing school, she'd married the boyfriend she had intended to cheat on with Wickham.

Wick had left that little detail out of the story he'd told earlier this morning. Georgiana hadn't fancied herself in love with him. She had set out to use him as practice to snare the trust fund baby of a man her parents had paired her with once they knew of her conception. Wick had never been anything more than a servant to her, a hired hand for a domestic service he wasn't interested in performing.

Rich women, like rich men, always got their way in the end. Which was why Wick had no crisis of conscious in using and deceiving them. He'd thought his little red Flame had been different. He was right; she was different. She wasn't rich.

As Wick pulled onto the training grounds where the rodeo was housed, he spotted Denny. The young man was smiling and grinning at a few girls who crowded around him. The buckle bunnies, as the riders called girls who hung around the rodeo, likely came to slum it with a bull rider for the day.

Wick marched up to the man, grabbed him by the collar, and slammed him into the nearest wall. The bunnies promptly scattered.

"Did you do that on purpose?" Wick growled.

"Do what?" the younger man squealed.

Wick and Denny were both contenders in the world of rodeo. Denny was the favorite to take first place this weekend. The two had a friendly rivalry and a casual friendship, but Wick hadn't thought the man would purposely try to trick him like this.

"You led me astray." Wick tightened his grip on the man's collar.

"Astray?" Denny wheezed.

Wick wanted to roll his eyes and curse this younger generation. Weren't there spelling bees any longer? Did all of today's youth think a thesaurus was some kind of prehistoric dinosaur?

"You led me down the wrong path when you pointed out that heiress."

"You mean Emma Woodhouse? I told you I got us both an invite to her birthday party."

"You pointed to the redhead when you said her name."

"The redhead? Oh, you mean one of the Bennett girls? Now that's a cherry I'd like to—"

Wick slammed Denny against the wall again. Despite the man being a bull rider who got thrown off a raging animal as part of his job description, Denny's eyes rolled back in his head at the force of Wick's assault.

"What is your problem, man?" he said, though it was more of a pig's squeal as Wick tightened his hold on Denny's shirt collar.

"Don't you ever speak like that about her," Wick snarled.

"Which one?"

"Any of them."

Wick opened his hand and let Denny fall to the ground. The man crumpled like yesterday's smelly socks thrown into a hamper. But then Denny straightened, the steel of a bull rider returning to his spine.

Denny's face, which was always contorted into a mischievous smile, morphed into indignation. "What's gotten into you, man?"

What had gotten into him? That redhead had. Even now, the thought of any man sniffing around that flaming firebrand of a woman got Wick's hackles up.

"She's just a girl." Denny gave Wick a shove in his chest.

Wick's fist curled into a tight ball. He was set to cock his right arm back when he heard a sultry voice behind him.

"Save it for the bulls, gentleman."

He didn't want to turn to the owner of that voice. Already too much of his life, too much of his livelihood, was under her thumb. If she told him to jump, his wallet would ask how high. She'd told him to stop the violence he so blindly wanted to take out on Denny. But Wick knew that if he did, he'd be even further indebted to Verine Petska.

"You're just the man I was looking for," Verine drawled in her Eastern European accent.

Wick had never learned exactly what Slavic country she was from. He hadn't asked, and she'd never bothered to volunteer the information. Conversation wasn't something she ever asked of him.

"I need to get out of here," said Wick, giving both Verine and Denny his back.

Before he could get away, that claw-tipped hand reached out to him. Wick came to a halt, knowing that with one flick of her wrist, Verine could slice through his chest with a single, sharp fingernail.

"You can come back to my office trailer," she drawled,

making the Cs in her words into harsh sounds that hurt his ears. "There are things I need to… discuss with you."

Wick recoiled from her touch. "I mean, I need to get out of here, out of the rodeo."

"Too bad you're still under contract. And you owe me a lot of money."

Verine flicked a button of his shirt open. It was the second button from the top. Lydia Bennett had flicked the first one open. When his red-headed Flame had done that, Wick's body had lit on fire from her touch. When Verine did it, it left him feeling ice cold.

Ice cold had been his modus operandi since his eighteenth birthday. He hadn't felt any hint of heat when a woman touched his body since then. He'd forgotten he was even capable of warmth. Until last night.

"Come along, stallion."

Verine said the S like the hissing of a snake. It had always made Wick shudder. Only this time, he didn't bother hiding his reaction.

"How is it that I owe you money when I'm one of the draws at this two-bit rodeo?"

Verine had inherited the rodeo from her late husband. As she had been a pin-up model in the seventies and a trophy wife all during the eighties, she had no idea how to keep the organization afloat when her elderly husband passed away and his children, who were all the same age as Verine and had even less interest in working, left it to her in his will. Most of the riders didn't excel at the sport, and many injuries had abounded from lack of skill. But the crowds still came, because Verine had a knack for picking the handsomest, most showy riders out there.

"You're a prize, you know that." She patted Wick on the chest again. "But since you haven't won any competitions in a year, and I've been footing your bill, you owe me."

Wick rubbed at his temples. He knew all this. For the first few years in the rodeo, he'd raked in the cash by winning. Then he'd gotten hurt, and the wins became fewer and farther between.

Verine had been there in the last couple of years, offering to take care of him. It had been what he'd known all his adult life. Rich women finding him attractive and offering to put a little sugar in his bowl in exchange for a bit of his attention.

When Verine reached for him again, Wick held still. But his mind was consumed with the memories of flaming red hair that had instantly soothed him. A fiery red kiss that had been so sweet and all-consuming. He'd finally found a place where he wanted to kick up his boots, and it was with the wrong woman.

The touch of Verine's razor-tipped fingers was like standing still in a raging fire. But he couldn't afford to pull away from her. He barely felt it around the cold seeping in beneath his skin.

CHAPTER THIRTEEN

he *tap tap tapping* that echoed through Lydia's room should have been the sound of progress as her article for the *Capitol* wrote itself. But it wasn't her fingers gliding furiously over the keyboard of her MacBook Air as the inside scoop about the rodeo poured out of her. Instead, it was the sound of her foot tapping against the wood floor as she looked over the top of her laptop and out the window.

Wick had left forever ago. Lydia missed him as though he'd been gone a year. Even though she'd only known him for less than a day.

In truth, it had only been two hours since Wick had left. Two hours, thirty-seven minutes, and… Lydia glanced at the clock at the top right of her laptop. Unfortunately, it didn't count seconds. Still, she felt each second weigh on her heart, piling onto the very real ache there as she sat gazing out the window like a lovesick fool.

How could she miss someone so terribly that she'd only known for one day? For less than one day. They'd met yesterday in the evening, and it wasn't quite the afternoon yet.

Lydia had seen Wick under the fluorescent light of the Pemberley ballroom. She'd seen him under the moonlight with his face tilted up at the stars. And she'd seen him at dawn under the soft haze of the morning sun. She couldn't decide which vision of her beloved was most dear to her. The fact that she'd have a lifetime with him to make up her mind absolutely thrilled her.

She wanted to see him now in the afternoon sun. Closing her laptop, Lydia reached for her phone. Her thumb froze over the circular button that would bring the device to life.

Should she call him?

Would that appear too needy?

They were just starting this relationship, after all.

But they had both pledged forever.

Maybe she should text instead of call?

Lydia pressed her thumb to unlock her phone. When she tapped on her Contacts app, her thumb froze again as she realized she didn't even have his phone number. He was her fiancé, the man she was going to spend the rest of her life with, and she didn't have his phone number.

Her heart, which had been fluttering at the notion of connecting with him again, went light. She felt slightly dizzy from the weightlessness in her chest and the breathlessness in her lungs. Caught between the feelings of anxiety and anticipation, a wave of giddiness settled on Lydia's shoulders. She threw back her head and laughed.

Lydia couldn't wait to tell Wick this story. She felt certain he'd get a laugh out of her antics himself. But that would have to wait until they came face to face again.

When she got the giggles out, she ran her thumb over the face of her phone again. This time she did tap on the screen to call someone.

"Hey, girl, hey," said Emma.

"You will not believe what happened to me last night."

"Oh, I know exactly what happened to you last night."

"Nunh unh, there's no way you will guess this."

"You went off with George Wickham."

That brought Lydia up short. Even though Lydia was the one with the gossip blog, Em seemed to always know everything that was happening in Austen Valley. Often before Lydia did. Much of what went into Lydia's blog was secondhand information she'd gleaned from her best friend.

"How do you know about me and Wick?"

"Because people saw the two of you talking in the ballroom and saw you leave with him. Everyone's talking about it."

Lydia pressed her lips together after hearing that bit of gossip. She wasn't used to being the talk of the town, even though she liked to be present at the center of any gossip. She preferred to be the one shining the light on scandals, not standing directly in the spotlight of one.

"Everyone's saying George Wickham is a womanizer," Emma was saying.

"He is not."

Well, actually, Wick had told her that he was. But he'd used the past tense. Now that they were together, he'd put all of that behind him.

"They said he has something going on with the old lady who runs the rodeo," Emma said, as though she hadn't heard Lydia's initial protest.

Lydia had nothing to say to that. She didn't know who the owner of the rodeo was. She hadn't asked that question in her journalistic interview of her fiancé. She didn't think it was true. But she couldn't know for sure. She couldn't really know anything for sure.

"And I've heard some rumblings that he tried to seduce poor Georgiana Wickham."

"He didn't seduce her!"

Emma definitely heard her that time. There was a pause on the line. One where Lydia could imagine Em's perfectly plucked brows had risen to the baby hairs of her hairline. Her glossed lips would be rounded in the shape of an O as she peered down at her gem-encrusted phone case.

"He didn't seduce her," Lydia said in a more neutral tone. "She came on to him."

"I don't doubt that. I've seen the man. He's hotness on a stick. Even if he is older."

"He's not that old. He's still in his twenties."

"You sound a little emotional, Lyddie. Not like an objective journalist. I told anyone who was talking about the two of you that you were doing a story on the rodeo, and that's why you went off with him."

That was true. Or it had been true. The blank screen behind the closed laptop would call Lydia a liar on that front, though.

"Don't tell me he seduced you, too?" Em was saying. "You're too smart for that."

"He didn't seduce me. He only kissed me."

Emma's gasp crackled through the line. It was so loud that Lydia had to lean back and hold the phone away. "No, Lydia, you didn't. You didn't fall for a guy like that."

"A guy like what?"

"He's a user. A gold-digger. He goes after women with money so they can be his sugar mama."

"What you're saying is he wouldn't come after me because I'm poor?"

"I didn't say that, Lyddie."

"But that's what you meant."

Lydia looked down at herself. The skirt she was wearing

was another castoff of Emma's. Lydia had rescued it from Em's Goodwill pile and handed it to Jane for an alteration. Now the only thing Lydia wanted altered was taking the fabric off her body.

"He's not like that," Lydia said, standing and tugging at the skirt. "Because if he was, he wouldn't have asked me to marry him this morning."

"You spent the whole night with him?"

The censure in Emma's voice made something settle in Lydia's belly. The sensation held her in place, leaving the altered hand-me-down, trapping her legs from moving forward.

"Oh, sweetie." There was a syrupiness to the condemnation in Emma's voice. "He used you. He's not going to marry you."

Lydia wanted to shout that he hadn't used her. He hadn't taken any liberties, despite her trying to shove them all into his hands. But her mouth wouldn't form words under the weight of Emma's judgment. The way Emma talked about what had been the most beautiful night of Lydia's life somehow cheapened the experience.

"Don't worry, babe. When I get my hands on him, he's going to regret ever taking advantage of you. Do you hear me?"

"Em, I gotta go."

"Lydia? Lydia!"

Lydia hung up the phone.

First Darcy with his disdainful glare. Then her sisters with their dubious inquisition. And now her best friend with her pitying accusations.

If they weren't going to be happy for Lydia, then forget them. All she needed was Wick. That and his phone number so that she could call him.

CHAPTER FOURTEEN

$\mathcal{W}$ick shut the hotel room door behind him. The steam from the shower followed him out the exterior door, needing to escape the four walls as much as he needed to. Once in the afternoon sun, the rays dried up the remaining drips of water that clung to his skin. Even though he'd washed, he still felt Verine's claws on his skin.

He left the hotel lobby and walked down the street. There was no direction he cared to go. He let the wind blow at his back. He let the sun guide him forward. His leg protested at every step.

He felt the weight of the world on his shoulders. He knew that climbing on a bull this weekend would end his career, possibly even his life, with his injury. He also knew if he could hold on for eight seconds and win, it could be his ticket to freedom.

Eight seconds. It was the time he was allotted for most of the decisions in his life. It had only taken five seconds for Darcy to look between his precocious sister and Wick to make a decision. It had taken three seconds for Verine to size him up and offer him a place in her rodeo… and then turn around and make an offer he couldn't refuse. Last night, it had only taken one second for him to gaze across the crowded ballroom and pick out the wrong girl.

Wick's temples pounded. There was a dull ache at the base of his skull. No matter how many times he rolled his head around his neck, the tension and the tightness remained.

"Wick?"

Normally, when a woman called his name, he tensed. The sound of Lydia Bennett calling out to him set the tension back on its heels.

He knew it was her without having to turn around. He swore he could feel her presence. As she got nearer to him, the dull ache quieted. When he opened his eyes and saw her smiling that bright smile up at him, that flame of red hair billowing as she rushed to him, Wick forgot what pain felt like.

Without conscious thought, he reached for her. She came into his arms. Every ache in his body fled at the feel of her against his chest. The pounding in his head subsided at the scent of her. He brushed his lips at the underside of her chin and knew without a doubt that he could hold on to a wild stallion stampeding through the valley with her by his side.

Just a few hours ago, he'd thought this slip of a girl had been the answers to all of his problems. Now she was at the center of them. It wasn't her he needed to be holding; it was her friend.

Wick didn't let Lydia Bennett go. He couldn't bring himself to.

"I missed you," she said into his ear. She squeezed him tighter and kissed his temple. "Isn't that crazy? You've been in my life for only a day, and I've been missing you for the last four hours like I lost a limb."

Wick had no response because it was exactly how he felt.

Only not like he'd lost a limb. Like his broken, aching limbs had been restored to their former glory now that she was back with him.

The universe was punishing him. He'd finally found a woman he wanted to hold on to, and he had to let her go. He had to push her away.

He was going to push her away.

Any moment now.

His arms tightened around her as he pushed his nose deeper into those flaming red locks that he'd been thinking about while he'd showered and washed another woman's touch from his skin. In the end, it was Lydia that pushed away from him.

"I didn't have your phone number," she said, pulling back to look at him. "I was going to go by the rodeo—"

"No, don't do that."

The alarm on her face at his barked order quickly morphed into amusement. "I wasn't trying to be a stalker."

Wick pulled her back to him, locking his arms at her lower back. "I don't think you are."

If he was honest with himself, he would admit that he was on his way to go and find her. His car keys were in his back pocket. He'd been headed to his Mustang. He didn't have a single doubt that he would've ended up at the Bennett Ranch. What he did doubt was whether or not he'd pull up to the house and go in and find her. There was still the matter of his crushing debt.

When he didn't acquiesce to Verine's demands, she'd all too quickly reminded him of just how much he owed her and how she owned him. She'd done that while running her clawed nails over the exposed bit of his chest. Wick still wanted to hop back into the shower to get any last remnants of her off his person.

"I just wanted to check in," Lydia was saying. "When you left, you were a little out of it."

"I was," he agreed, but he didn't expand on it.

Just like he hadn't expanded about what really happened between him and Georgiana Darcy. He'd long ago stopped trying to figure out where he'd gone wrong in the incident. Especially since it continued to happen to him again and again.

Rich women—all women really—looked at him as a commodity they could purchase, try on for a bit, and then discard when he was no longer useful to them.

Not Lydia. There was nothing she'd asked of him. Nothing she wanted. Except for the pleasure of his company.

"No one seems to be taking to our sudden engagement. Not my sisters. Not Emma—she's my best friend, remember?"

Wick cringed at the mention of Emma Woodhouse.

"Only my dad seems to like the idea."

Something tickled the back of Wick's skull at the mention of Mr. Bennett. Wick liked having the man's approval. But he knew he wouldn't retain it after he broke his daughter's heart. Which he'd have to do when he broke off their engagement.

There was no way he could marry her. Not when he'd bring her nothing but financial woe. She deserved more than that. She was such a bright light. He didn't want to tarnish her flame with his problems.

"Are you having second thoughts?" she asked.

This was his chance. He could say yes and have a clean break. But his only thought was that it had been too many hours since he'd kissed this woman.

And so he did.

Wick leaned down and pulled her to him. He kissed his fiery flame, and it was like he was being given sweet wine after marching through the desert. He kissed her, and it was like sitting at a decadent buffet after weeks of starvation. He hated his lungs when they demanded he come up for air. He could've happily suffocated on her lips.

"Is this your hotel?" she asked. "We could go in and..."

That doused cold water on his face. He couldn't go inside with her. He could not steal her innocence. Despite what others thought of him, he was not a debaucher of virgins.

However, if they were married, he could have her. And not just for a single afternoon of delight. He could have her in his arms for the rest of his life. Which made the thought of the rest of his life look bright for the first time in a decade. If Wick could figure out how to get out of debt, he could have this woman. He could feel this way for every hour of every day.

"I don't want to take you upstairs," he said. "I want to take you home, to our home, to our bedroom and never let you out."

The joy that spread across her face made his knees threaten to buckle. With that bright light of happiness, Wick finally recognized that there had been doubts lurking in her green depths. Likely from her friends' and family's skepticism.

"I can't give you what you deserve yet. But I will. In time. Right now, I need you to wait for me."

Wick expected a fight. At least a frown. His Flame smiled in complete acceptance.

"I love you," she said, placing her hand on his chest.

A sensation went through his body. It was like nothing he'd ever felt before. At first, he thought this was it; his body was finally giving out on him. When his heart started beating again after skipping not one but two pulsations, Wick realized what that feeling had been.

"You don't have to say it back," she said, patting his chest. "I felt your heart skip a beat. I know you love me, too."

Wick dipped his head to her again and took her lips. He only barely heard the catcalls of passersby on the streets. He ignored them all and pulled his Flame closer.

"I'm going to marry you," he said.

"Duh," she giggled. "I know."

CHAPTER FIFTEEN

"Okay, ease up on the clutch and—WHOA!"

Lydia grinned ear to ear as Wick reached for the Jesus handle at the roof of the car which hung just inside the passenger side door. When she shifted into the next gear, Wick's hand let go of the latch and punched the interior roof. When next she pumped the brake before the clutch, he reached out the open window and slammed down on the roof.

Her giggles of delight rang around the inside of the car, much like the rocks kicking up against the windshield. Her hair bounced around her pixie-like face. Her eyes were wide and bright with merriment.

The car had backfired twice when he'd climbed into the driver's seat. He'd apologized with a wince and made some excuse. In response, Lydia had wondered aloud if the car simply needed a woman's touch. She'd asked if she could give it a go. He'd looked at her, dazed for a moment before unbuckling his seatbelt.

When she climbed into the driver's seat and took off, the car hadn't backfired. Not once. Despite the hairpin turns she made or the couple of mix-ups with the brake over the clutch —it had been a minute since she'd driven a manual.

The car didn't make a wheeze of protest as she got her stick legs under her. It didn't cough up a splutter of protest as Lydia mishandled it. The gears didn't protest as she ripped through them faster than the engine caught up with the shift. And neither did Wick.

She thought he would demand that she stop. She was certain at any moment he would take the wheel from her and make her pull over. He did none of those things.

Instead, he brought his hand back inside of the car. He palmed the buckle of the seatbelt, pulling the strap and letting it zip back into its holder so that he could turn and face her fully. He reached out, not for the steering wheel. He placed his hand over hers on the gear stick.

Wick didn't force her to shift up or down. He didn't try to guide her one way or the other. He simply laced his fingers with hers and allowed her to maintain control of his most prized possession.

"I've never let a woman drive my car before."

He thumbed Lydia's knuckles. His gaze was on her fingers and not on the road. The look in his eyes was forlorn. Lydia downshifted and began to slow as she felt his mood shift.

"Most of the women I've found myself..."—he cleared his throat, still avoiding her gaze—"engaged with over the last few years have picked me up in their expensive cars and handed me the keys. They wanted to be driven around, but on their terms."

The sudden smirk on his face didn't fool her. There was pain behind that grin. The same pain she'd sensed when he'd told her the story of his dismissal from Pemberley over Georgiana Darcy's advances.

That's when she knew it. Emma couldn't be right about him. Her best friend had called the man Lydia was in love with a womanizer. Lydia was certain that it was the other way around.

"Driver's seat or passenger seat," she said. "Doesn't matter where I sit as long as we're together."

He looked up then, his dark gaze capturing and holding hers as they drifted slowly down an empty country road. His eyes had been so heavy when he'd looked up. In real time, she saw the fog clear as he looked at her completely open and vulnerable.

"When's your birthday?" she asked.

"June 25th."

"What year?"

"Why?"

"I should know these things about you. Your birthday. Your age. Your phone number."

"My phone number?"

"I wanted to call you earlier. Text you. But I didn't have your phone number. We're going to get married, and I didn't know how to get in touch with you."

Wick let go of her hand. He turned around and reached into the backseat. He came back with her purse. Lydia didn't protest as he dug around in the bag's belly.

He pulled out her cell phone, sliding his thumb onto the circular home button. When the device didn't recognize his thumbprint, he glanced up. "Password?"

Lydia hesitated. She let go of the gear shift and placed both hands on the wheel, keeping a steady speed as the truck passed her.

There was a grin in Wick's voice as he spoke. "You want enough details to steal my identity, but you're going to hesitate on giving me your password."

"It's not that."

"It's what then? Did you accept another man's proposal,

and he's texting you on here?" Wick held up her locked phone, waggling it between them.

"No." With a flick of her wrist, Lydia pulled over to the side of the road. She cut the ignition and then turned to face him. "My password is embarrassing."

"Now I have to know."

The man's grin was breathtaking. It not only stole Lydia's breath. It stole the secret password that neither her sisters nor her best friend had been able to guess to get into her phone. But she told this man sitting across from her as a passenger as she sat in the driver's seat of his car.

Wick snorted before he could press his lips together to hold in his laughter. Lydia slapped him on the shoulder. All that managed to do was loosen his lips, and a full-throated belly laugh spilled out.

"Remind me to put in our wedding vows that thou shalt not laugh at thy wife."

"Oh, Flame, I have a feeling we're going to be laughing every day of our lives together."

He typed in the password with only his thumb. He slid his arm around her shoulders and tucked her in. Lydia came from a close family in a small town, but she'd never felt so connected to another human being in her entire life.

"You're so cute," he said as he typed in his information.

"I'm twenty-one," she said. "People will think that's a little too young for you."

"I'm twenty-eight. People might think that's too old for you."

"I really don't care what people think."

"Me, neither."

Lydia tilted her head up. Wick's grin spread as he bent his head to her, the cell phone forgotten. She lost herself in him so quickly, so easily. It had barely been twenty-four hours, and she couldn't remember what life was like before she'd known the taste of this man on her lips.

A honking horn had them springing apart. A van with the logo for the *Capitol* newspaper whizzed by. The young delivery boy waggled his eyebrows at them as he zoomed past.

The sign on the retreating van, more than being caught making out on the side of the road, made Lydia flush. Wick chuckled again as he brushed his thumb over her cheek.

"You're going to have to get used to public displays of affections, Flame. I've been kept behind closed doors that…"

He stopped himself from talking, nearly choking on the words he held back. Lydia wanted to strangle any woman who had used this proud and beautiful man, leaving him feeling unworthy.

She cupped the sides of his face in her hands. She waited until his gaze met hers before she spoke. "We are going to make everyone in this town blush with our public displays of affection."

"I'm going to take care of you, Lydia."

"I'm going to take care of you, too."

His grin was small, but his eyes were bright with that vulnerable light again. Lydia realized then that she would do anything to keep that light shining. In fact, she was going to do her best to make it grow brighter.

She was going to expose this man. She was going to tell all of Austen Valley what a good man she had managed to capture. It would all be displayed for everyone to read on the pages of the *Capitol* newspaper. And she couldn't wait to watch his face as he read the paper when it came in.

When that same newspaper delivery boy delivered the paper to them next week, and Wick saw her story about him for the first time, it was going to be the best wedding present ever.

CHAPTER SIXTEEN

*L*etting go of Lydia's hand was proving harder than Wick expected. Releasing her lips from his mouth was even more of a task. Taking a step back from her lush curves was almost impossible.

They stood on her front porch. The sun had set, but the porch light hadn't come on yet. It didn't look as though anyone was in the house. He hadn't seen anyone in the fields when they'd pulled up. They were completely alone. Even if they'd been in a crowd, he doubted he'd have noticed anyone but her.

Wick had never craved a person before. He'd never felt he needed anybody. But his body felt at its optimal level when this woman was in his arms.

All his cares fell from his tired back. Optimism came to rest on his light shoulders. His chest puffed out with the need to prove his worth to her. He stood taller, any ache and upset simply having vanished from his damaged knee. Wick was certain he could move a mountain if she asked him to.

Was this love? He wasn't sure. He'd certainly call it devotion. Love seemed too light and fragile from the reality of his emotions.

Speaking of emotions, Wick's were getting away from him. His temperature was high enough to give mercury a rise. His heart was skipping beats. Looking down at her now as she smiled up at him, his heart thudded fast in his chest as a flush spread over his cheeks.

Love or a fever? Wick wasn't sure. It didn't matter. All he knew was that he never wished to be parted from her.

"Stay." She breathed the word against his mouth.

Wick's whole body shuddered at the suggestion. He could stay with her. Or rather, she could stay with him. He could take her back to his hotel room and lock the door behind them. The problem with that would be that they weren't the only things that would be locked in that room. His problems would follow him in there. He would not trap her with them.

"I can't." Wick stepped back from her, releasing her from his kiss and his hold.

"Why not?"

That frown of hers was going to be the death of him. Already, his feet were in motion to reclaim the inch of space between them. Before he could stop himself, his hands were reaching for her. He kept his lips in check, though. Instead of pressing into hers, his mouth rested against her temple.

It was a very small victory, but he'd take what he could get with his defenses so low.

"I want to do this right," he said. "I want to do right by you."

Lydia made a sound in the back of her throat. It sounded part snort, part chuckle. Wick found even that unladylike action endearing.

"Like you'd do something wrong?" she huffed.

He opened his mouth to tell her the truth, the whole truth. That he'd gone after her because he'd thought she was her heiress best friend. That he was up to his knees in debt. That his knee was likely to give out if he even dared to climb on a horse, let alone a bull whose aim would be to buck him off in under eight seconds.

"Well, if you're not going to spend the night with me," she said, "I'm going to make you regret it."

Whatever words that had been forming on Wick's tongue in a confession were gulped down in the face of Lydia's threat. "Make me regret it? How exactly?"

And then she showed him how.

Lydia pressed her supple body against his, and Wick forgot all about his past. She wrapped her hands around his neck and tugged his head down, making him not care about any future. She was his in the present, unraveling every part of him that he'd kept bound tight and away from the women that he'd allowed to use him.

Instead of taking, she gave. She gave him her smiles. She gave him her laughter. She gave him her trust. She gave him her heart.

The selfish man that he was, Wick took. He took it all. He bent down to scoop her up and into his arms. Before he could get a hold of her, his weak knee protested, and he wobbled.

It was that stumble that finally broke the kiss. She didn't appear to have noticed. She reached for the door handle and pushed the front door open.

"Try to sleep with that on your mind," she tossed over her shoulder before slipping into the house.

"Witch," he called after her.

As her feminine chuckles faded, Wick's resolve hardened. He leaned his head on the wood door, mostly for support as he gave his knee a moment of reprieve. Also, because if he removed his hands from the door jamb, he would immediately reach for that knob and follow his heart inside.

George Wickham had been a good boy growing up. But the day he turned into a man was the last he'd seen of any goodness. He'd had to look out for himself from that day forward. He'd had to look out behind himself, too, as the rich women with wandering hands were very fond of grabbing at him from that direction.

Moving forward, he had a choice to make. He could take a bull by its horns and possibly clear his debt, but he would never ride again. He might not even walk away from that ride.

Or he could spend one night with Verine and clear the decks. No harm would come to his body. He was certain that his soul would be tarnished when he returned to the woman he loved. But he could at least return to Lydia whole.

Wick stood at the door, just a foot away from what he desired most in the world. By the time he pushed away from the porch, he still wasn't sure which direction he should take. He nearly jumped out of his skin when he saw the figure looming over him from the bottom of the porch steps.

"I was just saying good night to Lydia," Wick insisted, feeling like he'd just been caught with his hand in the cookie jar. In truth, he'd had his hands all over the sweetness that was Lydia Bennett, and anyone looking closely would see that she'd left her sugary mark all over his face.

Mr. Bennett tipped up his worn cowboy hat. In the dim light, it was clear to see a bright smile on the old man's face.

"I want to reiterate that nothing happened the other night in the barn," Wick said, coming down the porch steps. "That is, other than a kiss."

Mr. Bennett chuckled. "You're a stronger man than I am, then. I couldn't keep my hands off of her mother on our first date. That woman was a spitfire. Lydia takes after her, you know."

The older man leaned against the porch railing and

looked off into the distance. Wick followed his gaze, tilting his head back and looking up at the stars. It was the same starry sky he'd lain beneath, with Lydia resting against his chest. Wick realized that that was the moment it had all begun; that was the moment his heart had thawed and began to beat solely for her.

"I intend to do right by her."

"I believe you do, son," said Mr. Bennett. "I believe you will."

"You don't even know me." Wick didn't tear his gaze from the stars as he spoke. The notion that this man might believe him, might take his word at face value, was another dream he dared not wish for.

"I know your kind. Reformed bad boys make the best husbands. Trust me, I know."

Wick smiled as he looked at the unassuming older man. Mr. Bennett shot him a wink. Wick recognized the mischievous twinkle in the man's eye.

"I'm not quite good enough for her," Wick found himself saying. "I can't afford to take care of her."

"I wasn't prepared to take care of my wife—or the three daughters that followed. But we do what we must."

Wick's chest had long since stopped its racing pattern. Its rhythm was steady. His muscles tightened, ready to spring into action.

"We do what we must," he repeated.

CHAPTER SEVENTEEN

Wikipedia had been Lydia's friend in high school. Those brief summaries of books and events and happenings which she could easily rephrase and use in an essay of her own were priceless. That was probably the reason the site didn't count as a source. The free online encyclopedia was sustained and fact-checked by volunteers. So in college, her professors had made Lydia and her trusty sidekick break up. Apparently, the crowd source site wasn't good enough to count as a credible source in news articles.

Still, there was a wealth of information she gleaned there about the rodeo. Like the fact that the word rodeo came from the Spanish *rodear* which meant to go around. There were some details that she already knew. Like the difference between rodeo clowns and bull fighters. But an article on etymology or the mention of those clown-like performers likely wouldn't cut it. Especially not when they weren't the most exciting nor the most attractive feature of the rodeo.

This feature had to be about the bull riders. Lydia knew that scandal sold best. But there was no scandal where Wick was concerned. Not today, at least. In his past, sure. And maybe their whirlwind courtship would turn a couple of heads. But there wasn't enough there for a couple of pages.

Sitting at her desk this morning, Lydia found herself writing an engagement announcement. Followed swiftly by details of their wedding plans. Then she drew up a list of destination honeymoon jaunts that were picturesque. That might delight the readers of her blog, but it was unlikely to satisfy the readers of a major paper.

She needed more. She needed something juicy. Picking up her bag and her iPad, she headed for the front door. If she wanted to be an investigative journalist, she'd have to go out and investigate.

"I'm headed over to Pemberley," she called out over her shoulder.

"I'll take you." Eliza appeared out of nowhere. She grabbed the car keys off the hook before Lydia could get to the door.

"Oh-kay," Lydia said, following her older sister.

Lydia climbed dutifully into the passenger side of the car. She buckled herself in, folded her hands in her lap, and waited for the admonishment she was sure was coming from her big sister.

Eliza was silent as she backed down the drive. She kept her own counsel as she began down the winding path that led to Pemberley. With one hand on the steering wheel, she ran the other hand over her jaw as she stared straight ahead, seemingly lost in her own world.

Lydia threw up her hands, impatient for the lecture she knew was to come. "All right, out with it."

Eliza frowned. She turned with raised brows, as though she'd forgotten Lydia was even sitting next to her. "Out with what? Oh, right, your new boy toy."

"He's not a toy. He's my fiancé. We're getting married. I'm sorry if you don't approve of him."

"Approve of him? I don't even know him. And neither do

you. It's just another reckless and impulsive decision of yours."

"When have I ever been reckless or impulsive?"

"Like that time you went to Brighton with Emma."

"It's not like I knew there would be a regiment of soldiers there."

"No, but you didn't have to write a blog rating their pickup lines as you flirted with each of them."

Lydia opened her mouth to defend herself, but then she paused. That blog post had gotten her the highest hits and website visits before her post on Carlos. Maybe she could do that again with the bull riders?

She was so engrossed in her plan that she hadn't noticed the car had stopped. Eliza was already climbing out of the driver's seat. Lydia scrambled behind her.

"You don't think about the consequences of your actions most times," Eliza went on as though she'd been carrying on the argument in her head. "Or how it reflects on the rest of our family and the ranch's reputation."

"Well, you're not going to have to worry about that for much longer, since I'll be moving out after Wick and I are married."

"Married?"

Both Bennetts turned at the low growl of Fitz Darcy's voice. The menace in his voice struck Lydia as odd, when the man rarely showed any emotion other than disdain.

"You can't be serious," he said, the disdain back and in full effect.

Lydia knew Darcy's opinion of her fiancé. She didn't care to hear it again. Especially from a man who didn't know the true character of his little sister.

"You barely even know the man," Darcy was saying to her. Then he turned to her sister. "I thought you'd talk some sense into her when you found out."

"Excuse you." Eliza tilted up her chin.

"You can't let her go through with this. Both of you barely know him."

"Don't tell me what I do or do not know." Eliza held up a finger and began to waggle it at him. "If my sister says George Wickham is the one for her, then that's all I need to know."

"It's a bad idea to entangle yourself with him, Ms. Bennett. He'll only break your heart."

Lydia supposed the words were for her, but Darcy's gaze was fixed on Eliza as he said them.

"I'm making the choice to entangle myself with him," Lydia said. "And he's *choosing* to entangle with me."

Darcy's brows drew in at that. The slight twitch in his left eye made Lydia wonder if he knew the truth of what had gone down between his sister and Wick.

"Don't presume to tell my sister whom she can be involved with," said Eliza.

"She has nothing he wants."

"What's that supposed to mean?"

"He chases after rich women."

"Are you calling us poor?"

"I…" Darcy ran a hand through his hair. Not a strand came out of place. There was a tremble in the fingers of his right hand as he scrubbed down his face. "That's not what I meant."

"Oh, I think I know exactly what you meant, Fitz Darcy. You think you're above everyone in this town."

Fitz took in a deep breath, then he let it out. He pressed his lips together as though trying to hold words in. Eliza wasn't done with him. But Lydia was done with both of them.

Having seen this particular battle play out time and again over the years between the two enemies who pretended they didn't want to be lovers, she turned on her heel in search of what she'd come here for. Distantly, she could still hear Eliza and Darcy arguing, but it wasn't about her.

Really, both of them needed to pay more attention to the young women they professed to be protecting. Maybe with a bit more guidance on their part, they'd get the results they were hoping for. Though Lydia doubted it.

Walking across the fields to where the rodeo tents were set up, she kept an eye out for Wick. She knew she could grab for her phone and text him. He'd put his number in under the heading *Dream Guy.*

Lydia grinned just thinking about it. He was her dream guy. Not because he was handsome and charming. Because he had taken one look at her and had believed in her. He'd listened to her. He'd thought her words and her opinions mattered.

What was dreamier than that?

"Watch out there," called a voice.

Looking up from the animal droppings she'd nearly stepped into, Lydia came face to face with Denny. His grin wasn't as big as it had been when he'd been flirting with Emma. But it was still pretty wide.

Perfect. He would be an excellent start to the article she would write.

"Oh, it's you," he said. "You're the cherry who's got Wick all twisted in a bunch."

"I beg your pardon?"

"You're the girl he thought was the heiress."

Denny looked Lydia up and down with a lascivious glance. She couldn't tell if he was undressing her or calculating the cost of her hand-me-downs. The skirt she wore today was one of Emma's castoffs. It was last season's straight off the runway. Em hadn't even worn it once, but it was one of Lydia's favorites.

"I think you're confusing me with Emma."

That was hilarious, as it never happened. The two girls looked as different as night and day. But men often tried to use Lydia to get to Emma. That was likely what Denny was trying to do now.

"I'm not the one who was confused. That was your boy, Wick. But don't be sad, honey. If he's dumped you for the heiress and her millions, you can let me comfort you."

Lydia had no clue what he was talking about. Denny was likely the one who was confused. Wick hadn't even met Emma yet.

Lydia stepped back from the young bull rider. She'd thought he was cute the other night, but clearly the guy wasn't all there where it counted. Likely too many throws from a bull.

ick walked into the training tent and looked up. The sky wasn't in sight under the high blue top of the cloth, so he couldn't even see the singular star shining brightly in the daytime. On the ground was mostly dirt, covered by a few patches of grass, and even more exercise mats.

Men in gym shorts were sprawled on the mats. Some were doing calisthenic exercises and Tabata. Others contorted their lean bodies into yoga poses. They could do that with their nineteen- and twenty-year-old bodies. Wick was the only one in worn jeans, boots, and a cowboy hat. That was the difference between today's bull riders and his generation.

Where Wick had had on-the-job training since he was a snot-nosed twelve-year-old who'd climbed onto his first steer, these kids had gone to bull riding camp a few years ago. Verine had picked the ones she'd deemed the handsomest high school and college athletes with no college or pro contracts and put them on a fake bull. If they could hold on for four seconds, half of the requisite eight second time to score, she kept them. Their ability to hold the female fans' attentions was far more important than their ability to hold on to a bucking bull.

Which also meant that their first priority was to keep their bodies in top shape for the onlookers. Wick was the only one with actual talent for bull riding. The truth in that could be seen on his medical records, which showcased a few cracked ribs, numerous concussions, a torn rotator cuff, and a knee that was going to need replacing in a few years… or sooner.

Just looking at the practice bull in the corner sent an ache reverberating up his body. His head throbbed. Even his teeth hurt. And he was only looking at a mechanical bull, not a real one.

"A little bird told me you're about to take the ride of your life."

Wick didn't bother to turn to face Verine. Just the pitch of her voice felt like a bull kicking at the back of his skull. He had no plans to hold on to that particular beast, not for another eight seconds.

With that realization, John Bennett's voice sounded in his head. Wick knew what he must do. "I'm not riding."

In bull riding, the actual riding wasn't the most dangerous part of the event. It was the dismount. Once free of the bull, the rider had to watch out for stomping hoofs and dodge horns.

Verine rounded on Wick. That predatory smile was sharp as it advanced into his personal space.

Wick warred with the notion of holding his ground or taking a step back.

"Then I take it you want to come to our other arrangement?" she purred. "I can stand for a little afternoon delight. Meet me in my office in about fifteen minutes. I just need to finish up this meeting."

She hadn't even bothered to say it in hushed tones. Good. Whoever the new rider in her office was, he would get an earful of what he was getting into and hopefully make a better decision. Better than what Wick had made of his life.

When he'd left Pemberley ten years ago, he'd cashed in that scholarship money. Instead, he'd lived off it as he went from rodeo to rodeo. The money was gone within two years.

That's when the predators swooped in. The only women he'd attracted had been ones who just wanted his body. The only men around him had been ones he was in competition with.

Not anymore. His Flame wanted him for who he was inside. She loved him. And her father seemed to like him. Her sisters… well, he'd win them over, eventually.

"You misunderstand me," said Wick. "I want out."

"There is no out, Wickham. I own that pretty hide of yours. The only decision you have to make is what you want to ride to pay off your debts."

"I'd rather work as a fry jockey than for you."

"You think because you're marrying money, you'll escape me? Well, I've got your pretty little fiancée in my office. Now she'll see what kind of man you are."

Wick's brows drew together. Lydia was in Verine's office? Had she heard all that? He'd wanted to tell her himself about his early intentions with her. He may have pursued her for ill gains, but that was in the past.

True, the past was only two days ago. But in those two days, he'd fallen for her. And for a man that had never believed in love, that was a pretty steep drop.

He would explain it to her. She would understand. She would forgive him. She had to because she loved him back.

But when he looked up at the woman standing in the doorway to Verine's office, he didn't see eyes full of tears. He didn't see brows pressed in distress. He didn't see flaming red hair.

"Emma?" he asked. "Emma Woodhouse?"

Emma glared down at him from a patrician nose. Even though he had a foot on the young woman, she still regarded him in that way of the rich that said he wasn't fit to grace the underside of her designer shoes.

She pointed a manicured finger at him. "You, outside."

She marched past him. A chilled breeze followed her out of the tent. For a moment, Wick held his ground. There was a part of him that felt safer staying behind with Verine than following the heiress out of the confines of the tent.

Outside, Emma stopped under a tree. She set her purse on the ground. Then she reached up to take first one and then another earring off.

"Explain," she said as she slipped out of her pumps and stood barefoot in the grass. Stretching her hands in front of her, she cracked her knuckles and then let her fingers ball into fists.

"Are we going to fight?" Wick asked.

Emma put her dukes up and hunched into a boxing stance. "If I don't like your answers and think you've been using my best friend, yes, we are."

Wick couldn't help the smile that stretched his lips. He liked this girl. If he'd had someone in his corner like Emma Woodhouse, there's no telling what he might have become.

She was a sight to behold. Her honey brown skin glowed in the sunlight. Her hazel eyes were as defiant as they were focused on her target. She was breathtaking. He didn't feel the pull to her that he felt to his bright Flame, but he felt a tie to Emma nonetheless. They had similar goals; they both wanted Lydia's happiness.

"I love her," Wick said simply. The words that had eluded him for all of his life easily rolled off his tongue.

Emma dropped her hands. She straightened, her eyes going wide, her smile shining brighter than the sun.

Wick relaxed, seeing that he had made an ally. But in the next instance, he doubled over as her fist flew into his gut.

"But you were going to use her to get to me and my money?"

"No," Wick wheezed as he clutched his gut. For a slender woman, she packed a mean punch. "I thought she was you, and I proposed to her to get to your money. Wait—"

Wick held up his hands as Emma advanced once again. Her fist was cocked, preparing to deliver another blow at those words. Wick scrambled a retreat, but his back met with the trunk of a tree.

"By the time I realized she wasn't you, it was too late. I was already in love with her."

"Wait? You really love her?" Emma, who had been bouncing on her toes like a fairy embodying the spirit of Muhammad Ali, came to a standstill. She still held her fists cocked, but she didn't advance. "I think I believe you."

"I'm a very convincing liar." Wick lowered his guard. "But I'm telling the truth."

"You're going to be my brother-in-law," Emma squealed, shaking out her fists like a dancer giving jazz hands.

"I don't think that's how it works."

Emma threw her arms up in the air. Instead of punching Wick, she threw herself into his arms. He had no choice but to catch her and hold firm. He was sure Lydia would not be pleased if he dropped her best friend.

He was right. Lydia stood at the other end of the tent. Wick could only just make out her features. She did not look happy. The only thing he could think to do was to squeeze her best friend tighter, to show Lydia that he had Emma in hand and would not let her fall.

Apparently, that was the wrong thing to do.

Lydia's gaze swept the length of his arms where he held Emma's torso tightly against him. His beloved's face contorted into something Wick hadn't seen from her yet: hurt.

But why was she hurt? He'd quit the rodeo. He'd come clean to her friend… but he hadn't come clean to her.

Did she know? Had Lydia found out that he'd mistaken her for Emma? That he'd been planning to marry her under the pretense of getting a fortune that he'd thought belonged to her?

Wick let Emma go. When he did, he registered the protest that had been happening all along in his injured knee. He leaned against the tree, trying to regain his strength. By the time he looked up again, Lydia was gone.

CHAPTER NINETEEN

$\mathcal{I}$t was true. What Denny had said was true. What Darcy had warned her against was right.

Wick had been after Emma all along.

Lydia hadn't wanted to believe. Not until she saw it with her own eyes. And even when she did, she still had trouble making it make sense.

There they were. Wick and Emma in an embrace. Those arms that had made her feel safe and wanted and special were wrapped tightly around her best friend.

Em looked up at him with a grin she reserved only for those she welcomed into her confidence. It wasn't the practiced half smile of disinterest. It wasn't a slight raise of her mouth as she looked for an escape. Lydia's best friend looked up at her fiancé with interest, with approval, with determination.

That's when Lydia knew she'd lost. Even if this had been a mistake, even if her eyes were deceiving her, even if there was some farcical explanation for what she was seeing, Lydia knew she'd lost him. No man had ever chosen her over

Emma. She had always been second to Em, existing in her hand-me-downs and charity dresses. Eagerly lapping up her friend's castoffs.

When Wick finally looked away from Emma and saw Lydia standing there, a shadow passed over his handsome features. His gaze roamed over her, looking her up and down. She knew what he saw: that she was nothing more than a poor copy of Emma. His brows drew together before his gaze got to her feet, and that's when she knew it.

He was not going to pick her. He was likely considering how he was going to let her down gently. Lydia couldn't stand to hear it, and so she took off.

"Lydia?" Em called.

But Lydia didn't stop. When she'd told Emma about Wick, her friend hadn't been happy for her. And now Lydia could see why. She'd wanted him for herself.

From the corner of her eye, Lydia saw Wick take a step, then a stumble, and come to a stop. He didn't chase after her. Of course he didn't. Why would he? He had Emma.

Every man chased after Emma. Lydia was just an obstacle in their way or a stepping stool to discard as soon as they got to their target. Lydia picked up her speed, but something had caught her on the arm. Or rather, someone. She whirled around to face her friend.

"Lydia, will you stop? Everything is all right now."

Lydia screwed up her features. Why would Emma think everything was all right? Lydia's world had toppled over. She was barely drawing breath, having been knocked completely off center.

"I'm sorry I didn't tell you what I was doing and went behind your back," Em continued. "But you're my best friend. Of course, I was going to look out for you."

Lydia tried to parse out the meaning, but Em's words made no sense. "What are you talking about?"

"I asked Knightly to look into George."

George? She was calling him George? Had Wick asked Emma to call him George?

"I had to know more about the man who proposed to my best friend after just one day."

"Because you couldn't believe anyone would fall for me so quickly."

It wasn't a question. It was a statement. But Em's brows screwed up. The bridge of her nose lifted like the curve of a question mark.

Behind her, Wick was making his way over. He hobbled on one leg, limping instead of his normal strong stride. Lydia's instinct was to go to him, to discover what was wrong. Instead, she dug her nails into her palms to resist that feeling. Wick wasn't coming after her.

"Then you found out it was you he was after," Lydia continued in Emma's confused silence. "And now you've taken him up on his offer."

"Yes. No. Wait." Emma put her hand to her brow and pinched it, but the crease wouldn't straighten out.

"The answer is yes," said Wick.

Lydia's chest constricted. Her ribs felt like they were squeezing her too tight. At the same time, the inside of her body felt entirely hollow.

"I thought you were her." Wick chucked a thumb at Emma. "I was after Emma for her money."

"And now you've figured out your error and you've seduced the right woman," said Lydia.

"No, Flame."

"That's not my name!"

All this time he'd been calling her that nickname was because he thought she was someone else. All around them, people stopped moving. All of their eyes took in the scene and looked at the drama unfolding. People would be telling this story for years to come.

"Lydia," Wick said quietly.

"Darcy was right about you."

Once again, Wick stumbled. His right leg wobbled as though it could no longer support his weight under the truth of her words. Because her words were fact.

Darcy had warned her that she wasn't the kind of girl Wick went after. He had predicted George Wickham would break her heart. And here Lydia stood with the organ in tatters, dressed in Em's discarded skirt.

She wished she could disappear away from the watchful gazes staring openly at her. She wished she could rip Emma's skirt off. She wished she could rip her heart out. Though that last part would have been no use.

Her heart wasn't where it was supposed to be. She'd given it to Wick the moment he'd flashed that smile at her. The smile that wasn't meant for her. And now she'd have to live in the shadows while the man she loved married her best friend.

Wick opened his mouth. At first, his upper teeth pressed to his lower lip, as though he was going to begin with an F sound. Perhaps to call her Flame? But then he gave himself a shake, likely thinking better of it.

Next, his tongue pressed to the roof of his mouth, as though preparing to make the L sound for Lydia. He was standing just behind Em. When he shifted his stance—to come forward? Perhaps to step closer to Em? Lydia would never know.

When he shifted, Wick wobbled again on that right leg. The movement silenced him. And he stood still.

That was all Lydia needed to see. It confirmed what she knew to be true. He'd made his choice.

"Lyddie—" Em began.

But Lydia gave a ferocious shake of her head. Whatever her former friend had to say, Lydia wouldn't listen. Instead, she took off running, determined never to see or hear from either of them again.

CHAPTER TWENTY

"*I*t's going to be fine."

Wickham's heart came to a full stop as he watched Lydia ran away from him. With each step she took, the ice quickly rushed into his chest. The shards made fine points aimed at the freezing organ, forcing his heart to continue to shrink. He made to step forward, but the ache in his knee stopped him. He knew that no matter how many steps he took, how fast he might get his wretched limbs to move, he would never catch her.

"She's never like this. I don't know what's gotten into her."

All around him, the crowd had grown. He didn't notice a single pair of eyes taking in the sight of him falling flat on his face while standing upright, while his insides turned to a winter wonderland.

Not Lydia's sister Eliza's accusative green gaze.

Not Darcy's denunciative dark gaze.

"Well, she is a Bennett. Those redheads can be a little hotheaded at times."

Wick had read somewhere that it was cold in the blackness of space. Made perfect sense that frost would rein in the absence of a star. His Flame moved farther and farther away from him, taking her light and her warmth until the bitter chill was absolute.

"But it's going to be fine. It's my fault, and I'm going to fix it."

That brought Wick up short. "Your fault?"

"I shouldn't have stuck my nose in where it didn't belong." Emma rubbed her pert little button nose as she spoke. "I have a habit of doing that, but I always mean well."

"Emma, no. This isn't your fault. I did this. I was going to use you; you realize that?"

"Pfft, as if." Emma waved the notion away as though it was ridiculous.

Wick wasn't sure if the *as if* meant that she never would have gone for him or that there was no possible way she would have let him use her.

"I'm going to talk to Lydia, but first I'm going to talk to that manager of yours and take care of your debt."

With that, the tall bulldozer of a young woman moved past him. She picked up her shoes and purse, letting both sling from her fingers as she walked. Her strides were purposeful and pointed. People moved out of her way as she passed with barely a glance at her. It was as though Emma Woodhouse expected the world to bend to her will.

The world obliged.

He did not.

Wick's knee didn't protest as he raced up behind her. When he caught her by the elbow, she glanced down at his hand as though it had offended her. He immediately let go, but he didn't let loose of the subject.

"I can't let you do that," he said. "I can't let you pay for my mistakes."

"Forty-eight hours ago, you were prepared to let me subsidize the rest of your life."

"Yeah, well, that was then."

"Let me guess." Emma stopped walking and rounded on him. They'd left the crowd behind and were at the entrance to Verine's office. "Now you're a changed man because you've fallen in love with my best friend?"

Emma stood with her hands cocked on her hips. For such a young woman, there was a wizened lift to her arched brow. Wick tilted his head back and turned his face up into the sun, preferring the star's glare to hers.

There was a red streak in the sky. It almost matched the color of Lydia's hair. Almost. It wasn't quite as vibrant.

"That's exactly why I'm going to do it," Emma declared. "I've been given all this money through no sweat off my own back. Unfortunately, a lot of people work hard trying to get into my good graces to claim a part of it for themselves. Lydia's never done that. She's only ever wanted to be my friend. I have to pretend I'm going to throw something away before she'll accept it."

"But I'm one of those people who wanted to claim your fortune, too."

"And you got it." Emma nodded. "You got the thing that is the most valuable to me. I'm not going to let her throw you away because she thinks you want me."

Wick ducked his head to hide the emotions welling inside him to be let out. He'd thought no one could love Lydia more than he did. Here stood his number one contender.

A poke in his chest sent him off balance. His co-conspirator morphed into an adversary with brows drawn and menace curling her upper lip.

"If you break her heart or screw this up, I will have you cut into tiny pieces and the bones buried in the valley. Do you understand me?"

Wick regained his balance in time to see something pass over Emma's features. She ducked her chin before he could catch it. When she lifted her head again, her dazzling smile was back in place.

"This is going to be my wedding gift to you," she said brightly, as though she hadn't just threatened to disembody him.

Within that threat was the answer to his problems. Yet he stood there, shaking his head. He held up his empty hands in a stop motion and took a step back on sturdy legs.

"I can't let you do that," he said.

"I'm not asking you."

"No, but you are meddling again."

Emma's glare returned. But Wick stood with the sun at his back. Though Emma's generous gesture was well-intentioned and went a long way to changing his mind about the rich, he couldn't accept it. The very thought of having another wealthy woman pay his way left him feeling hollow.

It didn't matter if he was drowning in debt. Lydia had been his air. Without her presence, he would still sink.

"I'm glad I mistook her for you," he said.

"Me, too." Emma grinned. "I would've seen right through you. Whereas Lydia... she saw right into you."

Wick wasn't so sure that was true. If she had seen into him, then she had seen all the lies. Now he wasn't so sure she could ever look past that.

CHAPTER TWENTY-ONE

*L*ydia stared at the blank page. The cursor blinked back at her, unwavering in its opinion that she had no idea how to fill its confines. The cursor was right. Lydia was out of her depth.

This wasn't writer's block. It was imposter syndrome. Except she hadn't known that she was pretending to be someone she was not.

Or had she?

All her life, she'd wanted to be Emma Woodhouse. An only child, living in a mansion, filled with brand-new toys—not hand-me-downs—and no need to share them with anyone. A doting father. A watchful next-door neighbor, whose eyes may have started lingering just a fraction too long when Emma came of age.

Emma had always been good at sharing. With Lydia, at least. Lydia supposed when someone was as wealthy as Em, they didn't notice the crumbs they left behind that the less fortunate would lap up.

Only this time, Emma had been presented with a full

meal on a platter. No woman in her right mind would share George Wickham. At least, Lydia wouldn't.

She'd had him all to herself for two glorious days. She got to be the sparkle in his eyes. She could never look at him again now that he would see her for the dim cast-off that she would be in Emma's light.

Sheesh! She should start writing poetry again if she was going to sound this morose. She certainly had no right penning an exposé about anyone or anything. Not that she even had a single thing about Wick to expose.

She was the scandal in this tale. She was the fool who'd grasped too high. Now she was left empty-handed while Emma would luxuriate in the richness of his laughter, in the ambrosia of his kisses.

Yeah, Lydia shut her laptop and reached for her dusty poetry notebook.

She picked up a pen. Only to slam it back into the pen holder when she realized it had once belonged to Emma. All of her fancy pens had come from Emma's desk. Heck, even her laptop had been Emma's computer last year.

Looking around her room, Lydia saw that most things in here had either been scavenged from Emma's trunk, handed over to her still in the package, or purchased by Emma when they were out shopping together.

If she was going to stand by what she'd declared after running away from the happy new couple, then there was a lot of work to be done. Lydia pulled the trash bag out of the waste bin in the corner of her room and got to work. It was likely going to take her all day to purge any trace of Emma and Wick from her bedroom.

Wick wouldn't be a problem. He'd left nothing of himself behind. Nothing except his phone number programmed into her cell.

Well, that was easy enough. Lydia grabbed her phone and

pulled up his contact details. A squeak escaped her lips as she looked at the title he'd put his number under: *Dream Guy.*

She wished it had all been a dream. She wished she could simply go back to sleep and pick up where they'd left off. She did not want to be a part of this living nightmare for the rest of her life.

The plastic bag in her hand felt too heavy to bear. The phone screen blurred as tears welled. Her chest hurt and felt numb at the same time.

A knock at the door had the phone tumbling out of her hand. But not before Lydia's thumb depressed the delete key.

It was done. There was no way of reaching out to him. Wick was gone from her life.

"Lydia," called Jane's voice. "There's someone here to see you."

Just like that, hope sprung eternal. Lydia's chest relaxed, and her heart kicked into third gear. She tossed the trash bag to the side and swiped at her tears.

The brass knob turned and... Emma appeared in the doorway.

"Lyddie?"

The alarm on Emma's face made no sense to Lydia. She expected gloating after Em had claimed her new prize. She expected a pleasure-filled grin if Em had just come from kissing Wick.

Still kneeling, Lydia slumped back down onto her haunches. Then she let her upper body collapse back against the bed frame, too tired to hold herself up any longer. The tears she'd just sucked back into her eyes she now let have free rein down her cheeks.

Toned arms came around her, carrying with them the familiar scent of an expensive fragrance that had been crafted just for Emma by a master perfumer.

"Oh, Lyddie, what's wrong? What happened?"

What's happened? She couldn't be serious.

Lydia shoved Emma off her and sprawled away. She didn't get far in her small room. She backed up against the other side of the bed. The empty trash bag tangled around her ankles. Her phone sat face up between them.

Though she had hit the delete button on Wick's contact, she hadn't hit the confirmation button. The red yes and green no confused her. Shouldn't yes be a bright green?

"What did he say to you?"

Lydia's head jerked up at the vehemence in Emma's voice. She'd only ever heard that tone a few times. Once had been when Billy Rikers had told everyone he'd made out with Lydia behind the bleachers during a homecoming game. Emma had read the boy the riot act, and he'd been a pariah until he'd gone away for college—far, far away.

"No, I didn't talk to him," Lydia said through a sniffle. "Unlike you, I wouldn't try to steal my best friend's boyfriend."

Or was Wick Emma's fiancé now? Lydia didn't want to know the answer to that question. She didn't want Emma in here. She wanted to suffer in silence.

Emma leaned away from her. She didn't gloat. She didn't grin. She looked down at Lydia with... That wasn't pity, thank goodness. Lydia would not have been able to stomach that particular emotion.

No, Emma looked at her with hurt.

"You really think I'm the type of friend that would try to steal the man my best friend was in love with?"

The censure in Emma's voice brought Lydia up short. What did Emma have to be disapproving of? Lydia was the wronged party here.

"No, I don't think you'd try to steal him," said Lydia. "Only because you wouldn't have to. He came to you. I was just a mistake."

"Lyddie-"

"Stop calling me that!"

Emma pursed her lips. It was clear she had more to say. It was even more clear that her patience was being tried. Emma was not used to having others tell her what to do.

Lydia got her feet under her and hoisted herself up onto her bed. "I'm done being second to you."

"When have you ever been second to me?" Emma asked from her place on the floor, kneeling beneath Lydia. "You've always been the first person in my world. My first friend. My best friend. I've only ever wanted the best for you."

Lydia shook her head, but the words Emma was saying were penetrating not just her ears. They were penetrating her heart. Inside her chest, Lydia knew them to be true, which only served to make her head hurt.

"If you're going to take him, I want you to take it all back. The clothes, the pens, the computer. But wait—let me just upload my documents to the Cloud first."

"Lydia, what are you talking about? I'm not taking anything from you."

"I don't want your charity anymore."

"Charity? What charity? Anything I've ever given you was a gift because I love you."

Lydia shook her head, but still Emma's words made their way through her ears and into her heart. As the words settled in her chest, they tilted the scale to the truthful side.

"Lydia, you can't really think I'd take anything from you?" Emma sat on the bed and grabbed Lydia's hands in her own. "Especially not the man who is so deeply, head over heels, in love with you."

Lydia's gaze was foggy again. There were no tears this time. Just total confusion. "He loves me? He told you that?"

Emma nodded, a bright smile on her face as she brushed Lydia's curls from her forehead.

"But he thought I was you." Lydia couldn't stop the tremble in her lips when she said the words.

"Maybe." Emma shrugged. "He still fell for you. Not what you wear. Not what you write. Not who you're friends with. He fell for you."

Lydia's head fell forward. She squeezed Emma's hands, needing to hold on to the truth of her words. Her head felt light. Her chest, which had been numb and constricted a moment ago, suddenly opened wide. Her thudding heartbeats rang in her ears. The organ beat so loudly that the fluttering tickled her belly, and she let out a giggle.

"He loves me," she laughed out loud.

"He does." Emma's tinkling laughter joined her friend's.

The two continued to grasp hands as their bodies shook with mirth.

"But wait," Lydia said as her head cleared. "What were you two doing at the rodeo tent?"

Emma scrunched up her nose. Her lips pursed once more, like she was trying to hold something in. "You do remember that bit about me only ever wanting the best for you, right?"

"Em?"

"I'm sorry, Lydia. I was trying to help. But I may have meddled and overstepped just a teensy bit."

"Tell me everything."

CHAPTER TWENTY-TWO

The heat was sweltering in the high of the afternoon sun. Though Wick was indoors, the hot waves penetrated through the roof of the barn. Had he stared up at the sky just two nights ago and seen his future written in the stars?

Those stars were nowhere to be seen now. His bright future was dark. His hopes of love and freedom were suffocating since the star at the center of his universe had stormed off in a burst of flames.

He'd heard somewhere that the sun was in the midst of exploding. The star was dying as it gave sustenance and life to all it shined down on. Wick understood the sentiment. Inside his body, he felt all the lights going out. Though instead of feeling hot, he was left feeling cold.

An ember flicked to life when he heard the door of the barn squeak open. The intrusion let in a welcome gust of warm, humid air. Wick felt his heart give a tentative, cool thump. A second later, the organ sank back into the chill when he heard the tread of heavy boots climbing the steps.

"I didn't know you were capable of caring for anyone besides yourself."

"Leave me alone, Darcy."

"You do realize that this is my property and you're trespassing? Again."

Wick slumped back down on the hay. The dry pieces stuck him in the back and sides. His injured leg was propped up on one bale. It wasn't the most comfortable, but he wasn't about to move.

"If you're going to have me thrown off your property like a common criminal for a second time, you'll have to man up and do it yourself."

There was silence. Darcy was always silent. But there was something different about this quietude.

It wasn't filled with scorn. There was no disdain in the thin, compressed line of Darcy's lips. Neither of his brows were raised in a sneer. He looked down at Wick, but his gaze was neither prideful nor prejudiced.

"I was wrong," he said.

Wick jerked upright. His leg slammed to the floor, which rattled the ache in his knee. The pain was muted in the light of his shock.

"Come again?" said Wick.

Darcy did roll his eyes then. He looked away from Wick and let out a weary sigh before he continued. "I know Georgiana came on to you, not the other way around."

Wick got his feet under him and stood. These were words that would've knocked him down if he'd already been standing. He wanted to be on equal footing, to be sure he didn't miss any of them, and also to be sure he was hearing them correctly.

"I saw the way she looked at you." Darcy held up a finger. Along with its rise went one of those aristocratic brows. "I also saw other women—older women, married women—eying you."

"That wasn't my fault. I didn't do anything to lead any of them on."

Wick wanted to add *back then*. He didn't. He had the high ground right now, and he wasn't about to step down from it.

"You were no innocent," Darcy said.

"Maybe not. But I wasn't the villain either. You cast me in that role, and everyone believed you. I've been typecast ever since."

Darcy breathed another long sigh, this one through his nose as he kept his mouth shut. His gaze took Wick in as though he was looking at the man for the first time.

Wick held still, surprised he wanted to pass muster for this man whom he'd hated so much for most of his life.

No. Hate was a strong word. Dislike was better. Disappointed fit best.

"I still think I did the right thing in sending you away."

Nope, Wick was back to dislike. Hate was just a few feet away.

"Georgiana was determined to ruin herself with you. You would not have stood a chance."

Wick wanted to protest, but in that, Darcy was probably right.

"You would not have stood a chance with Ms. Woodhouse."

Darcy had the right of it there. Emma Woodhouse had seen right through Wick. It had been his luck that he'd initially looked past her to the flaming redhead who'd stood beside her.

"I would tell you to run from Ms. Bennett, but I can already see that you're stuck and don't stand a chance of freeing yourself from her clutches."

Wick wished he hadn't had stood up. His body remembered he was tired, weary, and cold. His knee dialed up the throbbing ache from his injury. He felt behind him for the bale of hay. He collapsed down onto it, stretching his leg out to offer it some relief.

Darcy sat down beside him. The man didn't slump. His back was as rigid as ever, his mouth still pressed in that thin line of condescension. There was a slight tremor in his hand before he pressed his palm into his knee.

"I get the feeling," said Wick, "that you know exactly I how I feel."

"What I feel is partly responsible for the predicament that you're in."

"With Lydia?"

"With Verine Petska."

"Are you going to offer to buy my debt from her like Emma?" Wick gave a violent shake of his head. "I'm going to have to decline."

He'd spent nearly half his life being preyed upon and preying on the rich. This next phase of his life he wanted— no, he needed to pay his own way. That included paying for the mistakes of his past in full. He just prayed that Lydia would come to respect him again once he was truly free.

"I'm not buying your debt," said Darcy. "I'm buying the rodeo."

CHAPTER TWENTY-THREE

The rodeo was packed by the time Em hit the brakes and found a parking spot on the converted lawn of Pemberley Ranch. There were Fords and Chevys and Jeeps as far as the eye could see. It would take them another fifteen minutes just to maneuver their way through the crowd and into the tented arena.

Lydia palmed her cell phone. Her thumb hovered over the call button, though she knew it was no use. Wick wasn't picking up.

"He's probably preparing for his ride," Em said as she rubbed her hand up and down Lydia's forearm.

"He said he was done riding."

What if that wasn't the only thing he was done with? What if he was done with her, too? She hadn't trusted him enough to stop and listen to him explain. She hadn't believed him. Just like when no one had believed him about Georgiana Darcy.

Whether Wick was done or not, Lydia had to get to him. She wasn't done with him. She never would be. They were only just getting started.

"Ladies and gentleman," the announcer's voice boomed over the loudspeakers. "Welcome to the annual Pemberley Ranch Rodeo Spectacular."

The roar of the crowd made Lydia wince. Not enough to close her eyes entirely. She was glad she didn't because that's when she saw him.

Wick stood in the lineup of bull riders. He wore a padded vest over his muscled chest. Leather chaps covered his strong thighs. His cowboy hat was dipped low on his head so that Lydia couldn't make out his expression.

She didn't need to. She felt the sadness radiating from him. She also felt the determination. Even if she called his name over the cheers of the crowd, she knew he wouldn't have come to her. Not in that moment.

She let Emma tug her into a seat on the raised bleachers. Lydia had no idea how she sat still for the first thirty minutes of the exhibition as she watched bull after bull throw off its rider within five seconds. One rider barely made it out of the gate before the animal spun and ejected him back to where they'd come from.

She'd had just about enough of the display and was preparing to race to the back to find Wick when his name was called. Looking again, she saw him; he was sitting there. In the chute. His powerful body straddled a literal raging bull.

Lydia's heart pounded so hard she was sure the organ would leap from her chest to face the bull head-on. In fact, she stood up, fighting her way to the front of the railing that separated the crowd of fans from the arena floor. In the sea of people, she knew there was no way that Wick would ever see her.

And then he looked up.

Their eyes locked. His nostrils flared. Lydia inhaled as

though she was breathing for him. He parted his lips and exhaled the shared breath. The corner of his mouth lifted in a grin.

In that grin was everything unsaid between them. Just like the night he'd shown her the stars, Lydia saw forever—their forever—in his face. She answered his grin with a brilliant smile.

Her smile must have stood as a beacon to him, an answer to a question, because Wick gave a nod of his head... and then he was off.

The bull shot out of the enclosure like a beast possessed. It kicked and bucked and turned, trying everything in its considerable power to get Wick off of its back.

Two seconds ticked past.

Wick held firm. His one hand was in the air. The other was white across the knuckles as he held on tightly to the rope.

Four seconds ticked past.

The bull bucked so furiously that Wick's cowboy hat went flying off his head and landed in the dirt. It got caught up under the bull's hooves and went flying again. This time, it sailed in two different directions after being rendered in half.

Six seconds ticked past.

Wick listed to the left, nearly losing his seat. Instead of going languid and letting his body relax to move with the bull, a jolt of steel went through his form. Instead of keeping a watch on the bull, his head lifted, and his eyes caught hers.

That half grin he'd offered her was full now. That's when Lydia knew that all was forgiven. He forgave her for not believing in him. She forgave him for believing she was someone else.

Lydia had come for him. Wick was riding for her. As soon as he dismounted from the bull, they would embrace and put this all behind him. What she failed to realize was that one does not simply dismount from a bull as they do a horse.

Wick's grip loosened. The bull's hind legs drew in for one more ferocious kick. And Wick went flying through the air.

CHAPTER TWENTY-FOUR

"*And* the winner is George Wickham!"

Wick had died and gone to heaven. He'd felt himself drifting there when he'd climbed on the bull. The moment he'd taken his seat, he'd known it would be his last ride. When he glimpsed the angel in the crowd, he realized it might be more than just his last bull ride.

"Eight seconds with an outstanding score of eighty-two out of one hundred!"

Of course, there had been pain at first as Wick's leg protested being mounted on the beast that vibrated with aggression. He'd almost called it off the moment he'd pressed his thighs into the bull's back in preparation for his ride.

Then he'd looked up and seen her.

"That puts our hometown hero in the number one spot, and he takes home the grand cash prize!"

Wick would have spotted his Flame anywhere in any crowd. That red hair was a beacon for him. It would always call him to a place where he could rest, where he could find comfort, where he could dream.

She was the only thing he'd dreamed about in his life. The sole star he'd ever reached for. She'd fallen into his grasp, and Wick would never let her go. Not even when he died. Even now, when he was at the pearly gates of Heaven, Wick still held on to Lydia's hand.

"Don't you dare die on me," she demanded as she squeezed his fingers.

He grinned up at his angel, so thankful that her face would greet him here. Her face was hazy. Not quite in focus. But he would never mistake that red hair. He reached his hand out toward her and groaned in pain.

"George Wickham, if you die, I swear I'll kill you."

"Ma'am, you need to get back. " Wick recognized the rodeo medic's voice. "No fans allowed, only family."

"She's my fiancée," Wick managed. Or at least he thought he said the words. Now that things were becoming clearer, the pain was settling in.

Everything hurt. Both his legs. His right arm. No—scratch that. His entire shoulder was on fire.

Maybe this wasn't heaven. Maybe it was the other place.

"You may have broken something," said the medic.

But if this was hell, what was a medic doing here? And Darcy? Were they his tormentors?

The medic shouldered his way past Lydia. Wick's Flame held her ground and wouldn't let go of his hand. He laced his fingers through hers. It was her touch that let him know that he was still here on Earth. Because just like yesterday, the pain went mute when her hands were on him.

"Ouch!" he yelped when the medic lifted his leg.

"We're going to need to get x-rays to be sure," said a medic.

"It's fine," Wick said. "If anything is broken, my girl can washi it together."

A surprise laugh escaped Lydia's pursed lips. "You're joking, so you're going to be okay. He's going to be okay, right?"

"It may only be a sprain, but with his history of injuries, he's never going to ride again."

Wick nodded his head in confirmation. "I'm never going to ride again."

"Why did you ride just then?" Lydia asked. "You said you were done."

Wick opened his mouth to respond, but another yelp of pain came out of his mouth. They'd rocked his injured leg as they lifted him onto the stretcher. In the transfer, his grip had loosened on Lydia's hand.

He reached for her again. She shouldered her way past one of the medics carrying him and retook Wick's hand. The pain was still there, but his focus was on the heat radiating from his love.

"I'm in debt," Wick confessed.

"I know. Em told me." Lydia rushed to keep pace with the men carrying him as they carted him off to a waiting ambulance.

"She offered to buy it, but I said no."

"I know that, too."

Wick groaned again when they had to break contact as he was lifted into the back of an emergency vehicle. Lydia climbed in behind him despite the look of protest from the medic.

"Fiancée," she growled.

The medic opened his mouth, but his words were cut short.

"Let her go with him," Darcy said in his quiet, aristocratic tone.

With that, the medic held up his hands. Between the fiery

redhead and the stoic autocrat, the man knew when he was beat.

Wick gave Darcy a nod of thanks. Darcy pursed his lips in obvious discomfort. Wick doubted the two would ever be bosom buddies, but the gesture was a start.

His attention turned back to Lydia. Wick stretched his fingers again, but his shoulder was aching too much to lift his arm to her. Lydia reached for him the moment the doors of the ambulance were shut.

"Darcy bought the rodeo and also my debt," he said as she ran a hand over his temple, instantly cooling the fever threatening there. "I'm going to be working for him again, as the rodeo manager."

"Then why did you ride?"

"I rode anyway because I needed to take back control and not have someone else do it for me."

"You were wrong there," said Lydia. "From now on, we do these things together."

"Agreed."

"You could've gotten crushed by that bull."

"This isn't a crush," he said. "I fell and got hurt. Now I have a deep wound. Kinda like what I always thought falling in love would be like."

"Is it as awful as you thought?"

Wick shrugged. "There's one thing I didn't realize about being in love."

"What's that?"

"The one you love, who loves you back, will kiss it better whenever you hurt."

Lydia's cheeks flushed with emotion. Her eyes sparkled, just like the stars that had proclaimed her his and him hers. She leaned into him, a small sigh escaping her lips as she did so. Wick drank in the scent of her before he took his taste.

The aches and pains in his body were real. But even more

real was the pounding of his heart, the rush of blood through his veins, the desire in his soul for this woman who had brought light and heat and love into his life. He'd fallen for her in just a few seconds. But he was prepared to hold on to her for the rest of his life.

*D*arcy lifted a brow at the headline of the article in the *Austen Capitol* newspaper. He'd felt for some time that the news organization was going the way of the cart and buggy, especially with its once-a-day delivery while the news constantly changed by the hour. Today, he held confirmation in his hand.

George Wickham's Wild Ride was splashed across the top of the physical paper. Darcy hadn't bothered to look at the online edition. Beneath the headline, the byline of the author proudly stated that the drivel was written by one Lydia Bennett-Wickham.

Lydia had certainly taken her husband's story and twisted it and turned it to make Wick out as a grand hero. The story was complete with a hometown boy returning to Austen Valley to triumphantly make his last ride in the rodeo. Sprinkled liberally throughout the lurid tale was the love at first sight romance the two of them had shared. Thankfully, there was no mention of Darcy's sister's name. Though Darcy did have a mention as Wick's new employer as the former bull rider now took the helm of the rodeo, which would make its permanent home in the valley.

It looked like George Wickham was a villain no more in the town's eyes. Darcy couldn't take any credit for it. It was all Wickham's wife's doing.

Darcy's gaze fixated on the byline again. It was the hyphen that annoyed him. He was far too traditional and believed a woman should take her husband's name. In all his years, he never would have imagined the name Bennett hyphenated with that of Wickham.

Jane Bennett, who'd recently married Darcy's close friend Carlos Bingley, had taken her new husband's name. Even Collin's wife, Charlotte, had taken his last name. He doubted the last remaining Bennett would take anyone's name.

He doubted Eliza Bennett would ever marry.

He doubted anyone would have the woman. What man could stand under that green glare as she dressed him down? What human could deal with those lush lips that never seemed to stop—

"There you are, Darcy."

Darcy's features tightened at the sound of his aunt's voice. He breathed into his nostrils and out the same way, demanding that his facial muscles relax. Any irritation would only lead to an even longer conversation with Aunt Catherine. The woman was a busybody and thought everyone's private lives were her personal business. Especially his.

"We need to talk about you marrying."

Darcy's lips pressed together into a firm, thin line. His gaze narrowed until he was squinting. His nostrils flared with distaste. His feelings on that particular business were written plain to see on his face.

As per her usual, Aunt Catherine ignored the warning glare he gave her.

"I've told you this before, Aunt Catherine. I'm not marrying."

"Then you'll lose your inheritance."

"We've discussed this." The thin line of his mouth parted to let out an exasperated sigh. "I'm a wealthy man without my inheritance. Take the money and give it to charity for all I care. You can't take Pemberley from me. I own it outright."

Before they were even born, his parents had put in their wills that both Fitz and Georgiana would need to marry to get into a trust set up for them. Georgiana had married as soon as she was legal. His cousin Collin hadn't escaped the edict and had married earlier this year. His union turned out to be a happy one.

"You don't seem to understand the full weight of your inheritance, my boy."

Darcy did understand the weight and the balance of his inheritance. There were a lot of zeroes in his trust. But not enough to force him into unholy matrimony.

"Fine." Aunt Catherine threw up her hands. "If you want to forfeit the Bennetts' land, then so be it. But you'll be the one to tell John Bennett, not me."

Darcy went completely still. His face was truly a blank mask. His emotions were all too stunned to make an appearance. "What do you mean?"

"I thought you said you knew what was in the trust," Aunt Catherine said, a sly smile on her wrinkled face. "The land that John Bennett and his family live on is legally yours. If you do not marry and claim your trust, they will lose their home, and they'll have to move away."

See the epic—epically bad—proposal Darcy makes to Eliza
in "How Ardently I Love You"
Book Four in the Pemberley Ranch Romances!

Having His Back

In Over His Head

Always On His Mind

Every Step He Takes

In His Good Hands

Light Up His Life

Strength to Stand

The Rangers of Purple Heart

The Rancher takes his Convenient Bride

The Rancher takes his Best Friend's Sister

The Rancher takes his Runaway Bride

The Rancher takes his Star Crossed Love

The Rancher takes his Love at First Sight

The Rancher takes his Last Chance at Love

The Silver Star Ranch Romances

His Pledge to Honor

His Pledge to Cherish

His Pledge to Protect

His Pledge to Have

His Pledge to Hold

The Flying Cross Ranch Romances

His Vow to Love

His Vow to Trust

His Vow to Treasure

His Vow to Adore

His Vow to Respect

His Vow to Defend

www.ingramcontent.com/pod-product-compliance
Lightning Source LLC
Chambersburg PA
CBHW071248150726
48001CB00018B/409